KU-422-433

Patterdale C... ...ool
Patt...
P...
CA...
Tel/Fax: ...383

GREG JAMES AND CHRIS SMITH

ILLUSTRATIONS BY AMY NGUYEN

PUFFIN

PUFFIN BOOKS

UK | USA | Canada | Ireland | Australia
India | New Zealand | South Africa

Puffin Books is part of the Penguin Random House group of companies
whose addresses can be found at global.penguinrandomhouse.com.

www.penguin.co.uk   www.puffin.co.uk   www.ladybird.co.uk

First published 2022
This edition published 2023

001

Text copyright © Greg James and Chris Smith, 2022
Illustrations copyright © Amy Nguyen, 2022

Page 236 additional illustrations © macrovector/Adobe Stock and © Happypictures/Adobe Stock

The authors and publisher are grateful to Coldplay for permission to use the lyrics from the song
'42' in the epigraph, written by Guy Berryman, Jonny Buckland, Will Champion and Chris Martin.

The moral right of the authors and illustrator has been asserted

Text design by Ken de Silva

Printed and bound in Great Britain by Clays Ltd, Elcograf S.p.A.

The authorized representative in the EEA is Penguin Random House Ireland,
Morrison Chambers, 32 Nassau Street, Dublin D02 YH68

A CIP catalogue record for this book is available from the British Library

ISBN: 978–0–241–47052–7

All correspondence to:
Puffin Books, Penguin Random House Children's
One Embassy Gardens, 8 Viaduct Gardens, London SW11 7BW

MIX
Paper | Supporting
responsible forestry
FSC
www.fsc.org   FSC® C018179

Penguin Random House is committed to a
sustainable future for our business, our readers
and our planet. This book is made from Forest
Stewardship Council® certified paper.

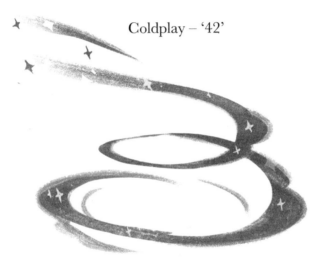

Those who are dead are not dead,
They're just living in my head.

Coldplay – '42'

CONTENTS

Prologue		1
1.	*Ghost Town*	43
2.	*The Super Ghost*	74
3.	*The Haunting of PANDAmonium*	94
4.	*Do You Believe in Ghosts?*	109
5.	*The Extraordinary Exploits of Doctor Extraordinary*	132
6.	*The Trojan Panda*	151
7.	*The Ghost in the Machine*	169
8.	*Hunting Pandas in Paragon Park*	202
9.	*The Shadow on the Wall*	219
9.5.	*Barry's Badger*	234
10.	*Hero Day*	242
11.	*Attack of the GIANT Giant Panda*	261
12.	*The Spirit of Doctor Extraordinary*	286
13.	*Giving Up the Ghost*	311
Acknowledgements		332

PROLOGUE

THE LAST STAND OF DOCTOR EXTRAORDINARY

Don't worry – the hero doesn't die at the end of this story.

He dies right at the beginning.

WAIT-
WHAT?

That's an unexpectedly sad opening for this kind of book, isn't it? I mean, it looks like a lot of fun – there's a load of pandas on the cover and everything. And then we go hitting you with that kind of sentence right at the start. Well, sorry. But this is a story about a ghost, and you don't become a ghost without . . . well, you know. But fear not. We'll be here all the way through to make sure things don't get too miserable. And the pandas show up a bit later – you'll love the pandas. They do a little dance; it's brilliant. Just wait.

But – as the old saying goes – before you meet the dancing pandas, you've got to get through the sad part. So strap yourself in for a dramatic prologue. Because, as this story starts, Paragon City is under attack. *Cue the stirring music.*

DUN DUN DUN DUN DUN DUDDA DUN DUN DUN DUDDA DUN DUN DAAAAAAA!

(It's hard to write stirring music down, but just try and imagine it, OK? Ooh, here comes a good bit.)

DUN DUN DUN DUN DUUUUN DUDDA DUN DUN DA DA DUN DUN DAAAAAAA!

You know Paragon City, right? With its tall sky-scrapers and busy harbour, set beside the sparkling waters of Lake Sunrise? Paragon City, famous for its excellent seafood and the scenic walks you can take on the slopes of the nearby Shadow Mountains? Oh, and it's also famous because it's constantly under attack from a very evil villain called Captain Chaos. But luckily Paragon City has a protector. Or at least it used to have one. Which brings us back to the sad thing that's about to happen.

Where were we? Ah yes. Paragon City was under attack. And this is the part of the story where the hero comes in, so please imagine the stirring music swelling to a climax at this point, as the camera pans across the surface of a lake, and the sound of jet engines builds.

DUN DUN DUN DUN DUN DUDDA DUN DUN BA-BLAAAAAARP!!!

SWOOOOOSH! A massive plane has just zoomed right above us. Everyone in the cinema goes '*Oooooooh!*' and bursts into spontaneous applause. The superhero has just made his big entrance.

Doctor Extraordinary glanced down at the controls of his supercharged plane, the gleaming black Extra-Jet, as it skimmed across the surface of Lake Sunrise, golden in the early-morning light. He adjusted one of his silver-edged black leather gauntlets (known simply as gloves to us non-superheroes) and nudged the joystick

forward just a fraction, bringing the jet's underside so close to the lake that the twin engines shot up a rainbow of spray.

That'll look amazing on the TV news, he thought to himself.

He reached up and clicked a button on the side of his large black flight helmet, which had a stylized letter 'E' on the front. 'What are we dealing with today, Holliday?' he asked calmly.

His earpiece crackled. 'Multiple blasts detected in the northern quarter of Paragon City, Doctor,' replied the voice of Professor Lana Holliday from the control centre back at Extraordinary HQ. 'I'm not sure what the threat is just yet, but we can't rule out . . . Well, the usual.'

'A giant robot?' said Doctor Extraordinary with a slight sigh.

'I mean, it might not be a giant robot on this occasion,' said the professor in his ear, attempting to sound cheery and convincing.

'Let's face it, Holliday. It's going to be a giant robot,' said the hero of Paragon City.

Bluey-white bolts of electrical current crackled round his gloved hands as he eased back on the joystick, and the Extra-Jet rose above the burnished lake surface. Suddenly the skyscrapers and bustling port of Paragon City were spread out before him with the dark mountains beyond. Through the windscreen he could make out a large smudge of green directly in the city centre – the huge expanse of Paragon Park. And, beyond the park, a thick inky plume of black smoke rose into the pure morning sky.

'It's always a giant robot,' muttered Doctor Extraordinary resignedly, gunning the engines to urge the squat jet forward and hurrying, as usual, to the rescue.

'Massive breaking news this morning, Susie,' said the young man in the leather jacket standing on the lakefront. 'This is Ben Bailey, reporting live from the shores of Lake Sunrise for *Good Morning Paragon*, and I can exclusively reveal to our *GMP* viewers that Doctor Extraordinary, the defender of Paragon City, is on his way to save the day once again.'

6

Ben Bailey, with his tousled dark hair and rugged good looks, was Paragon City's most fearless and successful roving news reporter. (At least that was what it said in his online profile, which he had written himself. This profile can be found at benbaileynews.com, which he had purchased, funded and kept updated on a daily basis.)

Ben gripped his microphone dramatically, staring seriously down the camera lens. 'Just a few moments ago, I witnessed the superhero depart from Extraordinary Island on his latest rescue mission,' he told his audience.

Back in the TV studio, Susie Carpenter watched the live footage from Bailey's camera operator as her lens zoomed in on a dark, distant dot above Lake Sunrise. Susie – three-times winner of Best Morning Show Presenter at the annual Paragon Television Awards – was very used to covering this kind of story. After all,

Captain Chaos tended to attack the city every few weeks without fail.

'It looks like Doctor Extraordinary's flying the Extra-Jet today, Ben,' she said, stifling a small yawn.

'That's right, Susie,' confirmed Ben Bailey, squinting theatrically into the dawn. 'We're trying to show you some exclusive breaking live-news footage right now – are you getting it?'

'Yes, we're seeing that here in the *GMP* studio,' said Susie, turning to the big screen behind her.

One of the camera crew let out an involuntary '*Ooh!*' as the feed showed the shiny black aeroplane dipping so close to the lake a trail of sparkling spray was kicked up behind it.

'Any idea what threat the doc is facing this morning, Ben?'

Most Paragonians (as they're known) simply referred to Doctor Extraordinary as 'the doc' these days. He'd been protecting their city for twenty years now – he was pretty much part of the furniture.

'Well, we know that he's chosen to use the jet rather than the Extra-Speedboat, the Extra-Cycle, the

Extra-Mobile or the rarely seen and frustratingly slow-moving Extra-Hot-Air Balloon,' the reporter replied. 'Meaning he wants to get there fast and airborne.'

'Giant robot, possibly?' asked Susie Carpenter.

Ben Bailey bridled. True, Captain Chaos did usually attack using a giant robot of some variety, but it wasn't really the done thing to pre-empt the news in this way. He'd been looking forward to a dramatic motorbike ride across Paragon City followed by a big reveal.

'No confirmation of what Doctor Extraordinary is up against so far, Susie,' he said irritably. 'But I can tell you that, as your roving reporter on the spot, I'll be bringing you the news first – live – right here on *Good Morning Paragon*.'

As he spoke, the Extra-Jet zoomed above his head, and he glimpsed one black-gloved hand held out of the window with the thumb upraised.

'For now, Ben Bailey, live on the lakefront, thank you,' said Susie Carpenter, gathering up her scripts and tapping them on the desk for no reason whatsoever. 'We'll bring you the latest on that possible giant-robot attack as we get it, but let's cross over to the *GMP* kitchen and see what Harriet's cooking up for us this morning.'

The camera cut to a grinning woman wielding a frying pan enthusiastically.

'Why, **HELLO**, Susie!' she bellowed.

'Change the channel! Argh! Change the channel immediately! Help! Emergency!'

With a triangle of toast clamped between his teeth and one scuffed school shoe hanging off his toes, Sonny Nelson hopped round the breakfast table on a frantic mission to find the TV remote.

'We're missing it! Quick! Find another news station!'

'Mmm?' Sonny's father looked up from his newspaper with an expression of mild surprise. 'What's going on?' He'd just come in from his night shift at the local police station, and his dark-blue officer's hat hung on the back of his chair. Rubbing his tired eyes with the palms of his hands, he looked around the small, cluttered flat wearily.

'Da-aaaaad!' wailed Sonny in frustration. 'We're *missing iiiit!* Doctor Extraordinary's on a rescue mission – it was live on TV and they've cut to the stupid cooking segment!'

'Ooh, is it that Harriet Wallace? I like her,' his dad said. 'What's she making?'

'Today, Susie, I'm going to be rustling up a cheese toastie with a difference!' burbled the voice from the TV. 'A turbo-toastie, if you will!' The studio broke into polite laughter.

'Cooking on TV is the most pointless thing ever!' complained Sonny, still hunting desperately for the remote control. 'Only one person in the whole world gets to taste the food! Ah! Got it!'

He discovered the TV remote behind a cereal box and started clicking through the channels, searching for a live feed of Doctor Extraordinary. As he did so, a deep roaring from outside began to rattle the windows of their fourth-floor flat.

'Sounds like a plane,' said Sonny's dad through a mouthful of toast. 'Hey!' he protested as Sonny dashed excitedly to the window. 'If you're not watching that, put *GMP* back on! I want to find out how Harriet turbo-charges her toastie.'

He grabbed the remote and changed channels as Sonny threw open the window and leaned dangerously far out, looking up and down the wide street. Early-morning traffic stretched away below Sonny in both directions. The roaring grew louder and louder.

'DAD! COME AND LOOK! I CAN SEE HIM! DAD!'

The gleaming ebony shape of the Extra-Jet was approaching, filling the street with the scream of its engines.

'I've already seen it on telly.' Sonny's dad was still glued to the toastie preparation taking place on screen.

'Now the secret to a really great toastie is to butter BOTH sides of the bread!' Harriet Wallace was shouting excitedly into the camera. 'DOUBLE BUTTER!' she added at top volume, opening her mouth so wide that her quivering tonsils were clearly visible on screen.

'But it's him!' cried Sonny. 'It's Doctor Extraordinary! He's about to fly past our actual window on his way to actually rescue the actual city!'

In case you hadn't realized, Sonny Nelson was Doctor Extraordinary's number-one fan. His bedroom was plastered with posters of his hero, diagrams of all the doc's various vehicles and maps of his headquarters on Extraordinary Island. Sonny's shelves were crammed with books about the doc's missions and back issues of the magazine *Extraordinary Weekly*, which was only available to members of his official fan club, the Sidekicks.

As Sonny leaned out, waving frantically, the Extra-Jet approached the window. Abandoning all thoughts of safety, he let go of the window frame so he could wave with both arms, frantically signalling to the passing plane. To Sonny's utter delight, the black-helmeted figure in the cockpit noticed him.

Doctor Extraordinary eased back on the controls, the twin-jet engines rotating to bring the plane into a momentary hover so he could give a quick thumbs up in the direction of the windmilling arms in a fourth-floor window. Then, with a screech, the jet lurched forward and away.

Shortly afterwards, there was a roar from below and a large crimson motorbike drove past, weaving rapidly in and out of the traffic. Roving reporter Ben Bailey was on the trail of the day's big story, his camera operator perched on the back of the bike and holding on for dear life.

As Sonny ducked away from the window, grinning from ear to ear, the Extra-Jet was already roaring over the trees, lawns and fountains of Paragon Park. Doctor Extraordinary allowed himself a brief look down. And, to be fair, it's hard not to fly above an enormous statue of yourself without at least glancing at it. Because that's exactly what was at the very centre of the sprawling park.

The statue stood with its legs apart, straddling a wide plaza surrounded by lawns, benches and trees, and behind it was a sparkling white concrete building with a gigantic letter 'E' emblazoned on its roof. This was the Doctor Extraordinary Museum – although, to be quite honest, he hadn't visited it since the day he'd conducted the official opening ceremony five years ago.

(Sonny Nelson, as you can probably guess, had a season ticket and spent hours every week gazing at the various exhibits – including the remains of the mysterious meteorite that had given Doctor Extraordinary his superpowers in the first place. And – as roving reporter Ben Bailey might say – more on that later. The large rock was kept in the very centre of the building in a special reinforced glass case, the strange crystals at the heart of the stone pulsating with an eerie blue-tinged white light.)

'Come in, Holliday,' said Doctor Extraordinary, tearing his eyes away from his own huge bronze doppelganger and steering the jet towards the plume of thick smoke. 'I'm almost there. Will have eyes on the threat in a moment. Stand by.'

He zoned out for a moment, gazing absently towards the distant horizon. After twenty years of constantly saving Paragon City, Doctor Extraordinary had recently been finding himself unable to shake off a slight weariness. He'd even, once or twice, caught himself dreaming about retiring and going off to save something else for a change. But somehow there was always a new threat the city needed defending against.

'Roger, Doctor,' replied the professor's calm, capable voice in his ear, snapping him back into the moment.

'Though I might as well tell you now,' the doc went on. 'It's going to be a giant robot. It's always a giant robot.'

(Just to put things in context even further for you, this was the fifth time that year Captain Chaos had attacked Paragon City, and all previous times she had done so using a giant robot. And it was still only 12 May.)

DOCTORS AND CAPTAINS – A QUICK NOTE

We just want to break into the story here because you're probably all wondering, What the actual coleslaw is going on? You've got a hero who's called Doctor Extraordinary, and a baddie called Captain Chaos. You've got your doctors and captains the wrong way round, you pair of absolute antelopes.

It's true that, up until now, most doctors in this kind of story have been villains. (See Octopus, Evil, No.*) But we've realized that in real life doctors are kind of amazing, so we've decided to reclaim the word 'doctor' by having a good character called Doctor something. Plus, doctors are generally great. Like really great.*

Similarly, most captains have been reasonably heroic. (See America, Marvel *. . . Actually, we can't think of a third one right now, but you get the general idea.* Birdseye! *There you go – that's another.) And, although captains are all right, we think doctors are better. So in this book the hero's a doctor, and the villain's a captain.*

17

If you think we've gone mad and you hate this idea, then please make this book into a smoothie and drink it. Otherwise, read on.

Yours,
Captain Chris and Doctor Gregory (or the other way round, depending on which one of us you like best)

End of quick note.

The Extra-Jet roared above Paragon Park, passing the tracks of the city's public-transport system, the Loop. This monorail coiled round the city on overhead lines, looking from its vantage point in the sky not unlike a large snake curled up between the buildings. Doctor Extraordinary pulled the joystick back to gain more height as he drew closer to the cloud of smoke, which he could now see was billowing out of the windows of a high skyscraper. And, clinging to the side of the building and shooting flames into the smashed windows from its gaping mouth, was a gigantic metal figure.

'Come in, Holliday,' said the superhero into his

mouthpiece. 'I have visual confirmation. It's another giant robot.'

The professor chuckled. 'Looks like I won the bet.'

'What?'

'Oh sorry,' she said apologetically. 'I was talking to someone here in the control room.' She cleared her throat. 'That's confirmed, Doctor,' she added in a more official tone. 'Giant robot attacking the city. Again. I'll inform the police department – should I tell them you've got the situation under control?'

'Why don't you contact the scrap-metal department while you're at it, Holliday?' said Doctor Extraordinary dramatically as he eased the jet into a hover above a smaller building next to the giant-robot-bedecked tower block. 'You can tell them to expect a big delivery. Of, er, scrap metal. Because I'm about to turn this heap of junk into . . .'

At this point, he realized he was about to say 'scrap metal' again, and he'd already done that twice. But give him a break; this was the fifth robot attack of the year, and he was starting to run out of puns.

'. . . into, erm, spare parts!' he concluded, smiling to himself with relief.

'Affirmative, Doctor.' Holliday was also relieved that the Doc had salvaged the cool superhero quip – they were always repeated on the evening news bulletin. 'See you back at HQ for brunch.'

'Start the pancakes, Holliday,' said Doctor Extraordinary confidently as he brought the Extra-Jet in for a smooth landing and pushed back the canopy with a thickly muscled arm. 'This won't take long. Although –' he spoke quietly to himself as he eased himself out of the pilot's seat – 'I can't help wishing now and then that Paragon City would save itself. Just occasionally. Anyway . . .'

He broke off with a sigh, vaulting neatly over the edge of the cockpit to land on the rooftop in the established hero landing pose – one hand in the air, the other fist on the ground, rear leg stretched out to full capacity. (DO NOT allow your parent or caregiver to replicate this pose at home; they'll probably do themselves a hamstring-based mischief or something. It's for heroes only.)

As the doc left the jet, the lights in the cockpit immediately blinked out, and the engines began to wind down. That's because the Extra-Jet, instead of running on normal aviation fuel, was actually powered by Doctor Extraordinary himself. That's right – one of his two incredible abilities was the mysterious electrical power that flowed through his body. He was basically a human battery.

And what was his other superpower? we hear you ask. Well, it's a slightly less unusual one, but just as useful. Doctor Extraordinary was the strongest being on the entire planet. To be exact, he was one of the two strongest beings on the entire planet. He was not only more powerful than a locomotive, he was more powerful than eight locomotives that had all been welded together to make some kind of incredible super-locomotive. Not that anyone would ever actually bother to do that; it's very silly.

Anyway, we're getting sidetracked again. Where were we? Ah yes, that's right. Our hero, Doctor Extraordinary, was on a rooftop, about to leap into action.

DUN DUN DUN DUN DUN DA DUUUUR!

He tensed his legs, squinting up at the giant robot clinging to the building above him, his brain calculating angles and velocity.

'HEY, DOC!' came a shout from across the street. Ben Bailey and his camera operator had taken up position on the roof of an office block opposite. 'You're live on *GMP*! Do you have any words for our viewers?'

22

Doctor Extraordinary fought down a slight irritation that he'd been interrupted in this fashion just as he was about to execute a very dramatic leap. But he mastered his annoyance – after all, it's very important to maintain good relations with the press if you're a superhero.

'There's no cause for alarm, people of Paragon City!' he said loudly in a reassuring tone of voice. 'Looks like Captain Chaos is up to her old tricks again, but there's no need to fear as long as I'm here.'

Ooh, that rhymed, he thought to himself. *I'll have to remember that one. Could make a new line of T-shirts.*

'This robot does look slightly larger than the previous ones,' said Ben Bailey, hoping to make his news story sound suitably dramatic so the programme didn't cut away to another cookery segment. 'Are you sure you can handle it?'

Doctor Extraordinary rose to his feet. 'Well, you know what they say,' he said with a smile and a raise of one eyebrow. 'It's not the size of the giant robot, it's the, er . . .' He paused, searching for a suitable quip and failing to find one. 'What I mean is,' he continued, 'it doesn't matter how large the robot might be. Doctor

23

Extraordinary is here!' And at this point he unfortunately decided to throw in a phrase that was about to become horribly ironic.

'NEVER SAY DIE!'

roared Doctor Extraordinary, preparing once again to leap into action.

With a powerful thrust of his supercharged legs, he soared into the air in a massive jump, landing squarely on the giant robot's shoulder with a clang. Reaching down, he ripped off a square metal panel and tossed it away like a Frisbee. Ben Bailey's camera zoomed in as the doc stood there, the morning sunlight catching his black cape with its silver edging, as it blew and rippled in a fresh breeze.

This must look amazing on TV, thought our hero. *Perfect time to bust out the catchphrase.*

('Dad! Dad!' said Sonny urgently, watching all this back at his flat. 'He's going to do the catchphrase moment!'

'He does that every time,' replied his father with a yawn.)

'Onward to the unknown!' said Doctor Extraordinary,

looking straight down the camera lens before he dropped out of sight through the robot's hatchway.

'Well, there you have it, Susie,' said Ben Bailey, stepping into position in front of the camera with the giant robot clinging to the skyscraper framed nicely behind him. 'Live on *GMP*, we've just grabbed a huge exclusive. An actual interview with Doctor Extraordinary during his latest rescue mission.'

'Thanks, Ben,' said Susie Carpenter back in the studio. 'We'll check in with you later. For now, let's see how those cheese toasties are coming on, shall we?' Giant-robot attacks weren't playing well with the viewers these days – it was rather old hat, to be honest.

Inside the chest of the robot, Captain Chaos sat behind a curved control panel, laughing wildly as she mashed levers forwards and backwards. 'Yes, smash, my pretty!' she was cackling. **'DESTROY! A-HA-HA-HA!'**

The captain, a tall woman with a long face and bright, wide eyes, was dressed in an outfit that was so peculiar it really deserves a paragraph all to itself. So here it is:

Captain Chaos's Outfit:
A Descriptive Paragraph

Imagine, if you will, a kid who couldn't decide which superhero to dress up as, so picked a small section of each different outfit and cobbled them all together into some kind of wacky mishmash. That's kind of the look Captain Chaos had ended up with. Her top had a tight-fitting yellow middle, a left sleeve that was baggy and bright neon pink and a right sleeve that was ribbed and dark purple. The thick belt around her waist was pure white, with a gold buckle in the shape of the letters CC. Her left trouser leg was a patchwork of rainbow colours; the right leg was bottle-green corduroy, but cut off at the knee. She also had on high yellow leather boots and – oh yes – a jester's hat. It looked as if a fancy-dress shop had been sick all over her. But, let's be honest, it's cool to discover your own style, and it kind of suited her. The outfit was the least villainous thing about her. The fact that she was, once again, trying to smash one of Paragon City's neighbourhoods into rubble was considerably more villainous.

(End of descriptive paragraph. Hope you liked it.)

26

Captain Chaos's menacing smile faltered as a voice sounded from behind her. 'Stop right there, you motley maniac!'

The supervillain spun in her chair, baggy left sleeve flapping, to see Doctor Extraordinary standing behind her, hands on hips.

'Doctor Extraordinary,' she said calmly. (It's an unwritten rule of being a supervillain that, when your arch-nemesis appears, you have to greet them by name.) 'I should have known you'd show up sooner or later,' she purred, once again following the villain playbook to the letter.

'BUT YOU'RE TOO LATE. ONCE I WAS YOUR LOWLY ASSISTANT.

NOW

I AM PARAGON CITY'S WORST **NIGHTMARE!**

A-HA-HA-HAAAA!'

Doctor Extraordinary was prepared for this little speech. It was the exact same one that Captain Chaos made every single time he thwarted one of her evil schemes, even down to the cackle at the end.

'Of course it's me,' he replied. 'It's always me, isn't it? Who else would it be? It's always you, and it's always me, and it's always – *always* – a stupid giant robot.'

He had grown a little tired of this same old narrative. Yet again, the idea of leaving Paragon City behind once and for all rumbled in his mind like distant thought-thunder.

'There's nothing stupid about this robot!' said Captain Chaos, stung. 'This is my greatest and most destructive creation yet! The Chaos-Bot Five!'

'It looks very similar to the Chaos-Bot Four,' said Doctor Extraordinary, frowning.

'How dare you?' shrieked his enemy. 'This one has flames!'

'I thought the last one had flames?'

'The last one fired bombs,' corrected Captain Chaos.

'Oh yes,' the doc said. 'I'd forgotten.'

'You're not taking this completely seriously, are you?'

Captain Chaos narrowed her eyes and swept her long hair away from her long face angrily. 'There's no point in my evil team of scientists designing a series of huge robots to attack Paragon City if the city's defender is just going to treat it like a trip to the funfair! This is serious! I am dangerous! Very, very dangerous!'

'Yes, yes, I know.' Doctor Extraordinary tried to focus. 'Let's get this over with, shall we?' He thought for a moment. 'Your giant robot is about to be turned into spare parts!' He'd used that quip once already, but he really was fresh out of ideas. 'Stand aside!'

'Never!' Captain Chaos snarled, closing in on her arch-enemy with her arms spread wide.

Outside, Ben Bailey filmed the giant robot twitching angrily and swinging to and fro on the building as the hero and his arch-nemesis wrestled across the room deep within its chest, slamming each other into the controls. They were evenly matched for the simple reason that they had the same superpowers. You may have noticed a few pages ago that we described Doctor Extraordinary as 'one of the two strongest beings on the entire planet'. Well, for reasons that will become clear in a flashback sequence later on, Captain Chaos was the other one.

'You won't stop me this time, Doctor Extraordinary!' the villain went on.

'You say that every time,' grunted the doc, pushing her back against the control panel and reaching for a large red button marked **SELF-DESTRUCT**.

'Don't you dare touch the **SELF-DESTRUCT** button!' said Captain Chaos furiously, pushing him away with a sudden burst of strength. 'You'll destroy my greatest creation!'

'Your fifth "greatest creation" this year,' corrected Doctor Extraordinary. 'And, besides, if you didn't want anyone to destroy it, why did you get your evil scientists to build it with a large obvious button labelled **SELF-DESTRUCT**?'

'Every evil creation must have a **SELF-DESTRUCT** device fitted to it,' said Captain Chaos, her brow furrowing with puzzlement. 'It's basically a legal requirement.'

'It absolutely is not a legal requirement,' Doctor Extraordinary pointed out, somersaulting over a chair and aiming a high kick at his enemy's chest. 'Although it does make my job a lot easier.'

'Not a legal requirement, then,' said Captain Chaos.

'What's the phrase I'm looking for? An unwritten rule, that's it! It's an unwritten rule that every evil scheme must have a **SELF-DESTRUCT** button. It's in every story I've ever read about villains.'

'Well, if you've read it in a story,' said the doc, jabbing at the captain with his gloved fists, 'then it's not unwritten, is it?'

'Look, stop arguing with me about grammar!' said Captain Chaos crossly. 'All I'm saying is . . . *don't touch that button!*'

At that moment, Doctor Extraordinary reached the main control desk with a flying leap and smashed his fist down on the red button.

Immediately, there was a hiss from the control-room doors, a red light began to flash in the ceiling, and a calm robot voice declared, **'Self-destruct sequence initiated. All exits have been sealed. Chaos-Bot Five will self-destruct in thirty seconds.'**

'What was that?' said Doctor Extraordinary. 'What did that voice just say?'

'It said Chaos-Bot Five will self-destruct in thirty seconds,' replied Captain Chaos. 'What did you expect it to say after you'd just pressed the large button clearly marked with the words **SELF-DESTRUCT**?'

'No, before that,' said the doc urgently. 'The bit about the exits.'

'Chaos-Bot Five will self-destruct in twenty-five seconds,' intoned the calm robotic voice.

'The exits?' said Captain Chaos.

'Yes! It said something about sealing the exits!'

'Hang on. I'll get in touch with supervillain support.' She pressed a button on the control panel. 'Come in, Castle Chaos. Are you receiving me?'

'This is Anna Podium back at the lab, Captain,' crackled a voice. 'How can I help you?'

'She's the real brains behind these robots,' explained Captain Chaos, looking up. 'She heads up the Evil Robot Construction Department at the castle. Brilliant scientist, completely brilliant. Ah, Podium,' she said into the microphone, 'we've just activated the **SELF-DESTRUCT** on the Chaos-Bot, and it said something about the exits. What's going on with that?'

'Yes!' The crackly voice from the radio sounded excited and, if we're being honest, more than a bit deranged.

'That's the most brilliant and chaotic advancement I've made in this latest robot. If the **SELF-DESTRUCT** sequence is initiated, all the exits are immediately sealed. It's impossible to escape, even with super strength like yours, Captain.'

'**Chaos-Bot Five will self-destruct in fifteen seconds,**' added the robotic voice.

'Are you joking, Podium?' raged Captain Chaos into the microphone. 'We're sealed inside a robot that's about to explode? What on earth is the point of that?'

'Well,' said Anna Podium, top villain scientist, giant-robot inventor and – it was now becoming clear – totally unhinged, 'it's designed to stop anyone activating the **SELF-DESTRUCT** mechanism. Obviously!'

'Don't you think,' shouted Doctor Extraordinary from the other side of the room, where he was tugging frantically at the heavy metal doors, which refused to budge even a millimetre, 'that it might have been a good idea to tell your boss that before she set off? Or have clearer signage?'

'**Chaos-Bot Five will self-destruct in ten seconds,**' interrupted the robot voice.

'Oh, this is just great, isn't it?' Doctor Extraordinary's face was sheened with sweat as he pushed desperately at the doors. 'I'm supposed to be making an after-dinner speech at the town hall tonight. The mayor's coming! What about overriding the **SELF-DESTRUCT** system?'

'Great idea!' Captain Chaos pressed the **TRANSMIT** button once again. 'Podium, can we override the system and stop the **SELF-DESTRUCT** sequence?'

'What would be the point of that?' came the answer. 'Not very evil, is it? Stop the **SELF-DESTRUCT** system just because you've changed my mind? That's the worst idea you've ever had.'

Anna Podium gave a slight snort that sounded very much like a badly muffled chuckle.

'Oh –' Doctor Extraordinary was about to say something rather rude at that point, but fortunately he was stopped by the robot exploding.

Ben Bailey had been broadcasting the whole thing from his nearby rooftop. 'We've seen Doctor Extraordinary drop inside the giant robot,' he told the viewers excitedly. 'He's probably reached the control room by now, and I

imagine he'll be wrestling with Captain Chaos, trying to activate the robot's **SELF-DESTRUCT** system.'

'And, Bwen,' asked Susie Carpenter back in the studio, through a mouthful of cheese toastie, 'bwhy boes Pwaptain Phaos bwild his bwiant bwobots with **PHELF-BESTWUCT** physsssstsms?'

(For the full effect, please read that sentence out loud with a mouthful of hot bread and melted cheese. Just be careful of any nearby soft furnishings.)

'Sorry, Susie,' said Ben in a confused tone. 'I didn't quite catch that question. You appear to have your mouth full of cheese toastie.'

He was feeling a little frustrated. He'd only been put back on air after he'd called the studio and pleaded that this was a major news story, and he was rather nettled that he was considered less interesting than a turbo-toastie. And now, to make it worse, the toastie was preventing him from understanding the show's host.

'Bwy bed –' Susie Carpenter paused to give a large swallow – 'I said,' she went on more clearly and less crumbily, 'why does Captain Chaos build her giant robots with **SELF-DESTRUCT** systems?'

'Well, Susie, it's really hard to say,' Ben replied. 'I suppose you might call it an unwritten rule of baddies. But there certainly will be a **SELF-DESTRUCT**, and . . . yes, in fact, you might be able to hear that?'

'Self-destruct sequence initiated!'

boomed a voice from the robot's mouth.

'I don't know if you caught that, Susie,' said Ben, 'but I can exclusively reveal – live – here on *Good Morning Paragon* that the robot's **SELF-DESTRUCT** sequence has indeed been activated.'

'We did hear that, Ben, thanks,' said Susie with a sniff. 'It was extremely loud.'

'ANY SECOND NOW,'

declared Bailey seriously, 'we'll see Doctor Extraordinary heroically leaping out of the robot before it explodes. Stay with us here on *GMP* for this breaking live-news story.'

'And more toastie secrets coming up with Harriet,' added Susie, worried that some viewers might switch channels rather than watch yet another live superhero rescue.

'ANY SECOND NOW,'

repeated Ben, 'the hero of Paragon City will appear.

Probably carrying the unconscious form of his enemy, Captain Chaos, who will escape to fight another day.

ANY . . . SECOND . . . NOW.

Just keep watching. He'll escape . . . before the robot explodes. That's what happened last time. And the time before that. And, indeed, the time before that.

ANY . . . SECOND . . .'

Bang.

The word 'bang' doesn't really do justice to the noise that interrupted Ben Bailey's live broadcast at this point. But it's the best word we can think of. You need to imagine a big bang, though. Like a really, really big bang. In fact, to do it justice, we really need to write the word 'bang' in such big letters that it fills an entire page. You know what? This is our book, and we can do whatever we want, so let's just make that happen, shall we?

That's better.

With a BANG so large that it filled an entire page, the giant robot exploded in a ball of orange flame. The heat was so intense that Ben Bailey had to duck down beneath the parapet of his rooftop, shielding his head with his arms, as a shower of tiny pieces of superheated metal pattered over him like really, really unpleasant rain. All over Paragon City, TV viewers watched in total disbelief.

In the *GMP* studio, Susie Carpenter had frozen with her mouth open. She'd been just about to take another bite of turbo-toastie, and a blob of hot cheese slowly detached itself from the sandwich and plopped on to the leg of her smart trouser suit.

'Susie!' her producer was screaming in her earpiece. 'Don't just sit there gawping! *Say* something!'

Susie Carpenter was a professional. Within a few seconds, she'd collected herself, arranging her face into a sombre-yet-approachable expression.

'The rest of today's programme,' she said seriously into the camera, 'will be a tribute to Doctor Extraordinary, the world's only superhero and defender of Paragon City, who has just –' She searched her brain for the appropriate expression. 'I'm not quite sure how to put this. Who has just . . . very sadly . . . been blown up inside a giant robot along with his arch-enemy, Captain Chaos.'

'That's great!' shrilled the producer's voice in her ear. 'Keep going just like that! Viewing figures will be through the roof! Look a bit more devastated!'

In his flat, Sonny Nelson was watching in complete and utter shock. He literally could not believe what he was seeing. Susie Carpenter was now dabbing unconvincingly at her eyes with a tissue as, on a screen behind her, a mushroom cloud of smoke expanded over the northern half of the city.

'What's going on?' asked his father, coming back into the room wrapped in a towel. 'Has he saved the day yet? Did he blow up the robot?'

'He . . .' Sonny couldn't quite believe what he was about to say. 'He did blow up the robot, but he was . . .' He swallowed painfully – it felt like something was stuck in his throat. 'He was still inside it.'

'What?' His dad gaped at him. 'Still inside the

robot? When it blew up? You don't mean he's . . . he's surely not . . .'

'Yeah.' Sonny Nelson steeled himself. 'He's gone.'

Phew. OK, that's the sad bit over with, we promise. From now on, it's silliness and pandas a gogo. And there's a good reason for all this, honestly. Look, if you're feeling a bit deflated by all that, don't stop reading now, whatever you do. Keep going through Chapter 1 and you'll feel a lot better. Guaranteed. We're sorry about this, OK? Here's a picture of a dolphin playing the flute to make it up to you. That's the prologue over and done with. Let's start the book properly, shall we? You're going to love it . . .

CHAPTER 1

GHOST TOWN

One morning, a month later, Sonny Nelson was awoken by Doctor Extraordinary falling on his head. Not the real Doctor Extraordinary, of course, for the obvious reason you've just read about in the prologue. But one of his many posters of the superhero chose that exact morning to fall off his wall. It was a large poster that hung directly over Sonny's bed, and showed the doc in a dramatic pose, looking out over Paragon City with his hands on his hips and his silver-trimmed black cape billowing out behind him. It was printed on thick, expensive card, and that being the case it was a fairly alarming and quite loud thing to have land on your face first thing in the morning.

'Argh!' squeaked Sonny, waking with a start to see Doctor Extraordinary's large, chiselled features looking directly into his own from a few centimetres away. He batted the poster away with his hands, and it flopped on to the bedroom floor with a wobbling rumble like a distant storm.

Sonny peered at his bedside clock, his tired brain wishing fervently that there was enough time for some more dreams before his alarm went off. But the clock rudely declared, in bright red numbers, that it was 06:58. Only two minutes until getting-up time.

Sonny rubbed his eyes and sat up. From around the room, numerous other Doctor Extraordinaries met his eyes. The walls were coated in posters, articles and clippings – even more so than there'd been a month ago.

WORLD WITHOUT HEROES

declared a headline above a moody black-and-white photo of the doc – it was the front page of a newspaper from the previous week, which Sonny had pinned to the back of his door.

Even though he knew he only had just over a hundred

seconds before the alarm went off, Sonny rested his head back on his pillows and closed his eyes. His mind drifted to that dreadful moment in front of the TV the previous month. *The moment*, he thought to himself, *that my world shattered*.

Images of the few days following that moment flashed through his mind – the endless news coverage, the articles in the newspapers discussing how the city would cope without its resident superhero. And, worst of all, the wave of crime and disorder that had swept through Paragon City since. His dad, along with the rest of the police department, had been completely swamped. Without a hero to constantly save the day, criminals had soon worked out that they had basically been given free rein to do what they liked. The only slight consolation was that Captain Chaos had also been blown up, so at least there weren't any more giant-robot attacks to worry about.

Sonny had watched helplessly as his dad came in from his shifts looking beaten down and exhausted, having spent yet another night trying – and failing – to keep on top of the spiralling crime rate. More than once, he'd caught his father looking at the posters of the doc with an expression that said, *Look at this mess you've left us to deal with.* Dad had even suggested taking the posters down.

'Come on, Sonny,' he'd said, trying to sound encouraging, even though he looked completely shattered. 'It can't be nice being surrounded by pictures of a . . . of someone who's not around any more. Why don't you pick something more cheerful?' But Sonny Nelson had refused. Because Sonny Nelson had a secret.

Despite his words to his dad on the day of the

explosion – 'He's gone' – Sonny had quickly realized that he didn't really believe Doctor Extraordinary was dead. He was Paragon City's one and only hero – he couldn't possibly be gone. He hadn't really been blown up inside that robot. It was all some kind of clever trick. Any day now, the doc was about to stage his dramatic reappearance.

As Sonny lay in bed, his half-awake brain painted a vivid picture of the Extra-Jet flying triumphantly over the city, with him and Doctor Extraordinary in the cockpit, waving to the people gathered below as confetti spilled from the surrounding windows, and the sound of wild cheering deafened his ears.

Suddenly he flailed upright as the alarm right beside his ear broke into a piercing wail – he'd been on the verge of dropping off to sleep again. He looked at the clock with a furious expression as he groggily groped on the floor for his dressing gown and slunk out of the bedroom.

'Disturbing news this morning as the crime wave continues,' a voice on the TV was saying as Sonny came into the kitchen. 'A month since Paragon City lost its defender, Doctor Extraordinary, the descent into chaos continues. A source within the police department has admitted to this programme that they are simply unable to cope with what they describe as a tidal wave of robberies and antisocial behaviour.'

'Turn it up, Dad!' said Sonny as he reached for the cereal, and – sighing slightly – his dad complied.

Officer Dusty Nelson looked, if anything, even more tired this morning – once again, just in from a night shift and still in his police uniform, which looked crumpled and stained. Police work had become a lot more difficult and dangerous over the last month. It's only when a superhero *doesn't* fly to the rescue that you properly realize how useful they are.

'She's not wrong about the crime rate,' Sonny's dad started to say. 'It's been a nightmare. Last night alone . . .'

But Sonny had drowned him out by thumbing up the volume on the TV, which was showing a large picture of Doctor Extraordinary with the words CAN WE COPE WITHOUT HIM? underneath. Then Susie Carpenter's face filled the screen.

'The mayor has announced that the Hero Day parade,

our annual celebration of Doctor Extraordinary, will still take place next week,' she went on. 'But critics are already saying that Paragon City no longer has anything to celebrate. Today, on a special edition of *Good Morning Paragon,* we're asking: can this city truly have a future now it no longer has a superhero to defend it? And, to begin our coverage, we're looking back at what can only be described as an *extraordinary* career.' She gave a small, self-satisfied smirk at this rather lame joke. 'Ben Bailey has this report.'

'Honestly,' said Sonny's dad. He had been working flat out every night to try and combat a surge in crime that was in danger of overwhelming the Paragon City Police Department. It was hard not to feel insulted to have the TV news openly accusing him and his colleagues of being unable to do their jobs.

'We're doing our best!' he went on, slapping the kitchen table in frustration. 'We can't all live our lives wishing that Doctor Extraordinary was still here. We've got to move on! I swear he's on TV more often these days than when he was alive.'

He harrumphed off to the bathroom, and Sonny

grabbed the TV remote and turned the volume up even higher.

'This is Ben Bailey for *Good Morning Paragon*,' the TV was now saying, and the camera panned down from a blue sky to show the reporter standing on the side of a wide valley. 'And this is the site in the Shadow Mountains where the story of Doctor Extraordinary began more than twenty years ago. Back then, of course, he was going by a different name. And it was to this tranquil valley that Doctor Xavier Arden came to investigate reports of a meteor strike. It was a day that was to change his life – and the lives of everyone in Paragon City.'

'Oh, not this again,' said Sonny's dad, coming back into the room after having calmed himself down slightly with a brief bathroom-mirror pep talk. 'You must know all this stuff off by heart now, surely? Weird crystals from space – he goes to investigate; there's some explosion or something. Nerdy scientist turns into a superhero; his assistant turns into his arch-enemy. Blah-blah-blah.'

'*Shh!*' Sonny held up a hand. 'I want to see it anyway!'

His dad shrugged and flicked the kettle on.

The TV picture changed, with an effect added to make

the colour look flickery and old-fashioned. The word
RECONSTRUCTION was now superimposed along
the bottom of the screen, as two figures came into view,
dressed in out-of-fashion suits.

'Doctor Xavier and his assistant, Catherine Case, came
to this crater, expecting just another routine examination
of a meteorite,' said Ben Bailey's voiceover. 'But, when
they got here, they discovered a cluster of crystals
completely unknown to science. The substance we still
know only as Q crystals. And, when they approached,
there was a burst of mysterious energy.'

51

The picture flickered back to the reporter in his leather jacket, now standing on the shore of Lake Sunrise.

'Before long, the hero known as Doctor Extraordinary had begun work on his headquarters, on the island you can see behind me.'

'Come on, Sonny, you'll be late for school,' his dad scolded him. 'Get in the shower, quickly!'

Reluctantly, Sonny turned away from the TV just as Ben Bailey was starting a description of the first time Captain Chaos had attacked the city, and how the newly created superhero saved the day.

When Sonny returned to the kitchen a few minutes later, hair damp from his shower, he saw that his exhausted dad had nodded off in his chair. The TV was still babbling away.

'So the question facing us all,' Susie Carpenter was now saying, 'is who will save Paragon City next time it's in danger?'

She leaned into the camera and narrowed her eyes. 'And the answer, it seems, is . . . NOBODY!' The *last* word, said in a dramatic shout, woke

Officer Dusty up with a start. 'Oh, you off?'
he asked.

'Yep,' said Sonny shortly, grabbing his bag.

'Tell Miss Abigail I'll pop in later once I've had a sleep,
OK? See if she needs any shopping doing.'

'OK, sure,' Sonny replied, raising a hand in farewell as
he headed out of the door.

'And be careful on the way to school!' his dad shouted
after him. 'It's not safe out there!'

'Yeah, well, whose fault is that?' said Sonny to himself
as he trailed down the corridor. 'If the doc doesn't
hurry up and come back, there'll be no city left to save.
Obviously the police aren't up to the job.'

'Is that you, Sonny?' came a voice through an open
doorway near the staircase.

Moving to the door, Sonny poked his head through.
The spacious corner apartment had high windows that
looked out over Paragon City. And sitting on a cushioned
window seat was an elderly lady with long white hair in a
thick plait that was draped over her left shoulder.

'Morning, Miss Abigail,' said Sonny. 'Dad says he'll be
in later after he's had a nap. See if you need anything.'

'Unless he's not up to the job any more, of course,' replied Miss Abigail, her eyes twinkling. As always, there was a pile of material in her lap – a huge patchwork quilt that she spent her days sewing as she looked out across the cityscape.

'Oh, you heard that, did you?' said Sonny, shuffling his feet with embarrassment.

'These old legs might not work so well,' Miss Abigail told him, 'but these –' she lifted a hand from her sewing to point at her ears – 'are still in fairly good order. You should go easy on your dad, you know. He's doing his best. He put up my picture of Walter – look.'

She gestured towards a framed photograph on the wall, showing Miss Abigail's late husband. He was a red-faced, smiling man, balancing on the deck of a small sailing boat, wearing a hugely proud expression while holding up a large fish he'd evidently just caught.

'He loved that boat,' said Miss Abigail wistfully. 'And he loved this city, too.' A distant police siren sounded from outside the window. 'He'd have been furious to see what's been going on.' She sighed. 'It's not easy to lose a hero,' she continued, fixing Sonny with her shining eyes.

'He was my hero, you know.'

'I guess I've lost my hero, too,' said Sonny sadly, thinking once again about the exploding robot.

'Have you indeed?' said Miss Abigail with a smile. 'Well, you'd better get off to school, hadn't you? Your dad's here if I need anything.'

With a wave, Sonny turned to leave.

'And keep your eyes open,' Miss Abigail told him as a parting shot. 'I find that more often than not a hero appears just when you need them.'

Thinking this was a reference to Doctor Extraordinary

staging an incredible comeback, Sonny smiled to himself as he trailed off and stomped down the stairs.

Back in her apartment, Miss Abigail picked up her quilt once more, looking out towards the distant Shadow Mountains with an unreadable expression.

At this point, you're probably thinking to yourself, *What's going on here? Sonny's dad's a police officer who also helps out the lovely old lady who lives next door. Why isn't this kid a bit more impressed? Why on earth have you made him the main character in your book?*

Well, before you give up on us completely – allow us to explain.

Firstly, you need to imagine what it was like working in the police department of a city that had a powerful superhero constantly protecting it. For twenty years, Doctor Extraordinary had been on hand – so, whenever a robbery was committed in Paragon City, the wrongdoers were neatly delivered to the cells, already tied up, and the stolen goods returned to their rightful owner. And there were several superhero quips along the way. Let's take a quick example to show you how it works . . .

SCENARIO 1:
CRIME COMMITTED IN A NORMAL CITY

One day, a lovely old man is walking down the street. He's clutching a bag of money – it's the weekly takings from his charming neighbourhood bakery, which he's run for the past fifty years. He's on his way to the bank to put the money in his account, and he's in a great mood because he's saving up to take his grandchildren on holiday. Suddenly a villain pushes him to the ground, snatches the bag of cash and rushes away down the street.

A kind passer-by helps the man up and calls the police. The police then investigate. They quite probably solve the crime, but only after a lot of hours spent looking into it. That's all very well, but have a think about this:

SCENARIO 2:
CRIME COMMITTED IN PARAGON CITY

One day, a lovely old man is walking down the street. He's clutching a bag of money – it's the weekly takings from his charming neighbourhood bakery, which he's run for the past fifty years. He's on his way to the bank to put the money in his account, and he's in a great mood because he's saving up to take his grandchildren on holiday. Suddenly a villain pushes him to the ground, snatches the bag of cash and rushes away down the street.

The villain turns into a side alley, opening up the bag to see what's inside. It's full of money! His mean face lights up with a mean smile. But, when he looks up, there's a figure standing in front of him, silhouetted dramatically by the street lights, with its hands on its hips.

'Stealing cash from lovely old baker?' says the silhouette in a dramatic voice. 'That takes the biscuit. I'm about to cause you severe pain. Which, although it's pronounced differently, is the French word for bread. There's nowhere to bun. You really should have used your loaf. Your opportunity to escape? S'gone. Scone.'

'Doctor Extraordinary, I should have known you'd show up,' replies the robber with a snarl, scrabbling in his pocket. He's going for his weapon, but before he can act, he's been punched to the ground by a gloved fist.

'Just lie down there and rest for a while . . . like dough during the proving process,' says Doctor Extraordinary, who is starting to run out of baked-goods references.

And, before he knows it, the mugger has been securely

tied up, dragged to the local police station and thrown into a cell. Doctor Extraordinary then delivers the bag of cash back to the kindly old baker, and just for good measure he pops round and visits his grandchildren, making them the coolest kids in school for at least three weeks.

All very lovely – but what did the police get to do? That's right: precisely nothing. Now remember this had been going on in Paragon City for twenty years. The Paragon City Police Department had pretty much nothing to do for two whole decades. They didn't even get to rescue cats stuck in trees – that was one of the doc's specialities. So all the police officers of the PCPD did was direct traffic from time to time, and the rest of the day they sat in their patrol cars eating takeaways, or they played endless games of pool back at the station – which, as you'd imagine, has a very well-equipped break room.

That might go some way to explaining why Sonny wasn't as proud of his dad as you might expect. Because, although Dusty Nelson had joined the police for the right reasons, and was brave and noble and all the rest of it, there just wasn't much for him to do. Until the past month, of course, when he'd been completely rushed off his feet. Add to that the fact that Sonny had once witnessed one of Doctor Extraordinary's daring rescues in real life, and from that day on had become a massive fan of the superhero. And, if you need a third reason, he was twelve years old, and it is completely forbidden, once you turn twelve, to think that your own dad is cool.

The next time Sonny was able to catch any of the TV coverage was on the train to school. Every morning, he climbed the metal steps to the station and took the Loop three stops to the very centre of Paragon City. Once he'd found a seat on the train, he tugged his phone out of his pocket and tuned back into the broadcast.

'Tomorrow the mayor will lay a special wreath at the gigantic statue of Doctor Extraordinary that stands in front of his museum in Paragon Park,' Susie Carpenter was saying. 'But questions are being asked about the mayor's leadership, and why the PCPD seem completely unable to deal with the spiralling crime rate since the loss of Doctor Extraordinary.'

Sonny glanced out of the train window at this point, looking down on a gloomy, graffiti-plastered street with black rubbish bags piled up on the corner.

This is a city that's missing its hero, he thought to himself. *But I know he's not gone. Not truly. He'll be back any day now, just wait and see. Imagine the celebrations when he turns up to save the day again.*

'*Paragon Central*,' said the robotic voice of the Loop's announcement system. '*Alight here for Paragon Park and the Doctor Extraordinary Museum.*'

The doors hissed open, and Sonny stepped down on to the platform, which was strewn with litter. Posters flapped in a chilly morning breeze, hastily pasted on to the walls.

CURFEW!
ALL PARAGON RESIDENTS SHOULD STAY INDOORS AFTER DARK.

said the closest one.

STAY SAFE, STAY HOME!

proclaimed another, as the train, which was spattered with untidy splodges and streaks of graffiti, lumbered into motion and disappeared off down the overhead line.

Sonny clanged down the metal steps to street level and

began to make his way through crowds of head-down, moody-looking commuters. What he hadn't told his dad was that ever since the explosion he made an unscheduled stop on his way to school each day. Every morning, he got off the train here to spend a moment alone thinking about his hero and wondering when the doc would stage his miraculous reappearance.

If the news reports and the posters hadn't already made it clear, Sonny's walk from the station to the park was enough to show him how much Paragon City was missing Doctor Extraordinary and his favourite pastime of 'saving the day'. More uncollected bin bags were piled on the street corners, and more graffiti was sprayed on the buildings.

There was a sudden disturbance in the crowd as a tall, mean-looking man grabbed a woman's handbag and tried to wrestle it away from her.

'Oy!' she protested. 'That's mine! You can't just take my bag!'

'Yes, I can,' countered the thief. 'Who's going to stop me? Doctor Extraordinary?' He laughed, ripping the bag out of her hands and sprinting off down the street.

A police officer on patrol nearby tried to give chase, but gave up before long, stopping not far from Sonny, bending over and panting desperately.

'You should have caught him!' shouted a passer-by indignantly.

'I'm a police officer!' the man told him, still struggling to catch his breath. 'I'm not used to this kind of thing! It's usually, you know . . .'

'A job for Doctor Extraordinary,' completed Sonny quietly to himself as he dodged round a crowd that had stopped to make sure the bag-snatch victim was OK, and headed on towards the park.

It was already a sweltering day, and Sonny had to swerve past clumps of joggers, dog walkers and rollerbladers as he passed through the tall iron gates into Paragon Park and followed the wide concrete path between ancient trees and wide spacious lawns. As he rounded a corner, the huge, gleaming figure of the bronze statue loomed up ahead of him. It showed Doctor Extraordinary looking out proudly across the city that had been his home, hands planted on hips in one of his trademark hero stances. The statue stood right in front of the large museum; its legs wide apart so people had to walk between them to get to the front doors, in the centre of a wide circular plaza surrounded by benches and a few stands selling drinks and snacks.

Despite the early hour, most of the benches were already full. Sonny looked around in disappointment. He'd been hoping for a few moments of quiet, but everywhere he turned there were people chatting, slurping coffee or munching breakfast. As he scanned the plaza, he even caught sight of someone dressed exactly like Doctor Extraordinary, with a black costume, black cape with the silver trim and everything, standing in the shadows among the trees behind the row of benches, staring up at the statue.

Sonny's eyes narrowed as he continued to turn in a circle. Something inside his brain was nagging at him. That figure in the trees really did look very, *very* familiar.

It really was a very authentic costume – much better than the ones you could pick up in Paragon City's tatty souvenir shops.

Sonny continued to turn, taking in more crowds of breakfasting Paragonians. His eyes passed the closed doors to the museum, and before long he was once again facing the strange figure standing stock-still back among the trees. Without really thinking about it, Sonny took a few steps forward, reaching up a hand to shield his eyes from the morning sun, which was already climbing above the lake.

He stared hard at the person dressed as his idol. It was, he realized, an uncanny impersonation. The thick black hair was brushed smartly up from the high forehead just the way the doc used to do it. The gloves were in place – that utility belt was incredibly detailed. *It must have cost a fortune*, thought Sonny, still walking slowly forward, almost in a daze. His heart gave a sudden leap. Was this it? Was this the moment Doctor Extraordinary had chosen to return? And he, Sonny Nelson, was here to see it!

A woman on a bench eating a croissant looked at him crossly as he came to a halt just in front of her, staring over her head. 'Do you mind?' she muttered.

'Sorry.' Sonny shook his head in confusion, but grinned with delight at the same time. 'But I think something incredible is happening. It's Doctor Extraordinary!' He pointed behind her. 'He's right here!'

The woman glanced irritably over her shoulder. 'There's nobody there,' she said curtly. 'That's Doctor Extraordinary there,' she added, gesturing up at the statue.

'No, not there.' Sonny pointed again. '*There!* On the grass! That guy, right there!'

Once again, the woman looked round. 'I don't have time to mess about,' she said, her face flushing with annoyance. 'Can't I have my breakfast in peace without searching for imaginary people? There's nobody there,' she repeated, punctuating this last sentence with three angry waves of her croissant, which scattered flakes of pastry like buttery confetti. She got to her feet with a theatrical sigh and stalked off across the plaza.

At this point, his eye apparently caught by the sudden movement, the man who looked exactly like Doctor Extraordinary lowered his head and glanced in Sonny's direction. His eyes widened. He checked over his shoulder, as if to make absolutely sure that Sonny was staring at him and not somebody behind him. Then he pointed to himself, mouthing something with an expression of complete shock.

'What?' Sonny, too far away to hear what the man was saying, cupped a hand to his ear. 'I can't . . . What are you saying?'

Abruptly, the man ran over to Sonny, skidding to a halt beside him. 'I said,' he repeated, 'can you see me? You can actually see me?'

'Of course I can see you. You're right –' Sonny began, but then stopped talking.

Alarm signals from his brain were clanging inside his whole body. Something incredibly weird had just happened, but what? It took him a moment to work it out. The man standing in the trees, who looked and dressed exactly like Doctor Extraordinary, had run over to talk to him, where he was standing, on the plaza. On the other side of the large, solid park bench that had been between them.

The man hadn't run round the bench. He hadn't

jumped over it.

He had simply run straight through it.

'Whoa,' said Sonny, backing away and holding up a hand. 'Whoa, whoa, whoa. What the actual heck is going on?'

'You all right, kiddo?' A woman jogging past had stopped and pulled one of her earphones out, looking concerned. 'What's the problem? You look like you've seen a ghost!'

With a shaking finger, Sonny pointed at the man who looked and dressed exactly like his hero. 'Please tell me you can see that,' he said.

The jogger squinted obligingly at what was, to her, a completely deserted park bench and a stretch of empty, sunlit grass.

'See what?' she asked. 'Birdwatching or something, are you? I can't see anything. Sorry. Just wanted to make sure you were OK. You looked pretty freaked out.'

'She can't see you!' Sonny said accusingly.

'Nobody can see me!' The man who really did appear to be Doctor Extraordinary wailed in despair. 'Nobody's been able to see me for weeks! You're the first person who's been able to. And you can hear me, too! You *can* hear me?'

'I can,' confirmed Sonny.

'Is this some sort of prank?' asked the jogger, smiling uncertainly and looking around. 'Am I going to be a meme or something? Have you got an earpiece in? Am I on TV right now?'

Sonny turned to face the woman, who was clearly going to be of no help whatsoever in this very unexpected situation. 'It's fine,' he told her. 'I'm fine. You can go. Thanks.'

With a final nervous wave in case of hidden cameras, the jogger replaced her earphone and trotted off.

Sonny planted his hands on his hips and rounded on the man. 'So is this a prank? What's going on? Why couldn't she see you? Is she in on this? How did you go through the bench?'

'He can see me,' muttered the man to himself, his face wearing an expression of such huge relief that his eyes actually brimmed with tears. 'He can hear me. At last. I don't believe it.'

'Are you Doctor Extraordinary?' demanded Sonny.

The excitement he had felt at the first sighting of his hero had drained away like dishwater, leaving him feeling as cold and hollow as an empty sink. Since the explosion, he had been convinced that the doc was about to stage a comeback. But the way he had run through the bench, and the fact that nobody else appeared to be able to see him, was causing a horrible suspicion to form in Sonny's mind.

'Of course I'm Doctor Extraordinary!' the man replied. 'Who else would I be?' He spread his hands wide and took a step back, indicating his black-and-silver costume.

'And you know the giant-robot attack last month?' Sonny went on. 'When I was watching you live on TV. I'm, like, your biggest fan, by the way. You waved at me from the Extra-Jet.'

'Oh, was that you?' said Doctor Extraordinary. 'Always nice to meet an admirer.'

'Never mind that now!' said Sonny crossly. Denial was swiftly giving way to anger. 'Did you or did you not get blown up inside that robot? Because I've been telling everybody that you're about to reappear and save the city – which, incidentally, is in a terrible state.'

'I did get blown up,' confirmed the doc. 'At least I think I must have done.'

'You actually did get . . . Hang on. I need to sit down.' His head suddenly reeling, Sonny sank on to the bench and plunged his face into his hands.

'Sorry if this is a little startling,' came a voice from above him, accompanied by a slightly embarrassed cough.

'Stop talking.' Sonny held up a pleading hand. 'You talking is not helping things. Just nod or shake your head, OK?'

He looked up to see the head above the smart black-and-silver costume nodding enthusiastically.

'Are you actually Doctor Extraordinary?'

Doctor Extraordinary nodded.

'Did you somehow escape from the robot and have you been living secretly in Paragon City for the last month?'

A sad shake of the head.

'So you were, in fact, inside the robot when it exploded?'

Nod.

'Along with Captain Chaos?'

A third nod.

'Which would make you . . . what? A . . . *ghost*?'

'I'm a ghost,' said the ghost of Doctor Extraordinary wonderingly, as if realizing it himself for the first time. '*A ghost*,' he repeated in a whisper.

'OK,' Sonny continued. 'So my next question might be a toughie. But it's this. How, how on actual *earth*, is this possible?'

The ghost thought for a moment. 'Do you know what?' he told Sonny seriously. 'I have absolutely no idea.'

CHAPTER 2
THE SUPER GHOST

'Stop following me!'

'You're the only person in the whole world who can see me! Of course I'm not going to stop following you!'

Sonny had glanced at his watch and, realizing he was about to be late for school, had hurried out of Paragon Park and away down the crowded street. It was so crammed with people that nobody seemed to notice him talking over his shoulder to the ghost who seemed intent on trailing after him.

'Look,' he said finally, stopping on a corner and planting his hands on his hips, 'you can't come with me. It's not . . .' He flailed his arms. 'It's not Bring Your

Ghost to School Day!'

'Well, who's going to know?' asked Doctor Extraordinary reasonably. 'In fact –' he warmed to his theme – 'maybe every day is Bring Your Ghost to School Day! You wouldn't know, would you? Perhaps your school's full of them.'

'My school is not full of ghosts!' said Sonny, more loudly than he'd intended.

Several hurrying commuters stopped and stared at him, one slopping hot coffee over her hand in surprise before she shrugged and carried on.

'Fine.' Sonny sighed. 'Come to school, then. Just, you know, try and keep quiet. And stay out of sight.'

'I'm a ghost,' said Doctor Extraordinary. 'I don't have a problem with either of those things.'

'Very funny,' Sonny told him. 'Just behave yourself. Try not to . . . I don't know. Try not to haunt anyone.'

'Believe me, I would if I could,' the doc replied. 'But it's been a month, and you're the first person who's seen or heard me. In fact, you're my very first haunting!'

As Sonny approached his school, his heart sank. He'd spent so much time in the park talking to the ghost that he was late. The wire gates slammed firmly closed with an ominous rattle as they sprinted towards them, and only a couple of final stragglers were visible, rushing to get inside before assembly – one of them tucking in her shirt as she held a slice of toast in her mouth.

'Right, this is where a superhero might actually come in useful,' Sonny told the doc. 'I'll get in trouble if I have to ring the bell and admit I got here late. This is where you leap into action.'

'You mean grab you and use my super strength to bound over the fence with the agility of a giant flea?' suggested Doctor Extraordinary excitedly.

'Erm, not quite sure about the creepy flea metaphor, but, broadly speaking, yes.'

'Then prepare for Mission School-fence Leap!' declared our hero. 'Onward to the unknown!'

Bracing his legs in preparation to jump, he attempted to grasp Sonny round his waist. And that's where the problem became evident. Because, instead of grasping anything, his hands simply passed straight through Sonny, leaving Sonny with a slight chill in his stomach as if he'd eaten too much ice cream too fast.

'Ah,' said Doctor Extraordinary, looking bashful and holding up a single gloved finger. 'Slight problem with the mission.'

'You don't say,' said Sonny with a sigh, reaching out and pressing the intercom on the gatepost.

A few minutes later, having been handed a note to give to his dad, Sonny and Doctor Extraordinary were racing towards assembly as the bell started to ring.

'We'll just make it,' Sonny said, panting.

Doctor Extraordinary congratulated him. 'Excellent! Mission accomplished!'

'It's not a mission!' Sonny told him as they sprinted down the passageway. 'It's just going to school.'

'When you're a superhero,' said the ghost from behind him, 'everything's a mission.'

'Well, your mission today,' Sonny told him, 'is to keep quiet and let me get through my lessons. Then we can try and work out what's going on, OK?'

'Mission accepted!' Doctor Extraordinary saluted smartly.

At this point, you might be thinking to yourself, *Why is Sonny being so rude to Doctor Extraordinary? I thought he was supposed to be his number-one fan. And now he's suddenly turned up as a ghost he's treating him like an unwanted uncle at Christmas.*

Well, remember that Sonny had spent the last month convincing himself that the doc was about to reappear to save the struggling city. Not as a ghost who couldn't actually use his main superpower because he was unable to touch anything, but as his actual real-life hero. It was going to be the ultimate twist in an incredible story.

Sonny had whiled whole hours away imagining how everyone else would have to eat their words and admit that he was the only one who'd kept the faith. So, when Doctor Extraordinary had run straight through that bench in Paragon Park, a realization had slammed straight into Sonny Nelson like a freight train full of electric eels. He had been the only one who'd kept the faith. He'd been stupid. He'd been wrong. The doc had died in the explosion after all. And what use was the ghost of a superhero?

'Won't your friends be really impressed that you're the only one who can see me?' said the doc at breaktime, jumping into Sonny's gloomy thoughts as they wandered aimlessly around the school playground. 'Where are your friends anyway?'

'I'm, ah . . .' Sonny scuffed a toe in a patch of dust, looking embarrassed. 'I'm kind of between friendship groups at the moment. At least that's what my dad says. I mean, I did have a couple of best friends, but we had a bit of a falling-out.'

'What about?' asked Doctor Extraordinary, perking up as he realized that saving Sonny's friendships could be a mission he might actually be able to attempt, as long as it didn't involve touching anything.

'Well, it was over you actually,' said Sonny, looking him in the eye, unable to suppress a wince as he remembered what had happened.

It had been the first day back after the explosion that had robbed Paragon City of its hero, and Sonny had hurried into school, eagerly looking forward to discussing the situation with his two best friends, Marcy and Jay. Together the three of them made up the school's chapter of the Sidekicks (the doc's fan club, if you'd forgotten).

Sonny's two fellow Sidekicks had already been deep in

conversation as he'd bustled across the school playground towards them.

'Yeah, they're kind of cool,' he could hear Marcy saying as he approached. 'Or what about getting into board games or something? They're really popular.'

'Morning, Sonny,' Jay had greeted him. 'We're just trying to work out what we can become number-one fans of next. You know, now the doc's not around any more.'

Sonny stopped in his tracks. 'What on earth are you talking about?' he'd asked, thunderstruck by this attitude. 'The doc's not *gone*. He didn't really get, you know . . . he didn't actually . . . he's not gone!' he repeated desperately. 'He's just waiting for the right moment to stage an incredible reappearance! I know it!'

His two friends regarded him with expressions that mingled pity, confusion and slight amusement. 'I told you he might have trouble taking it in,' said Marcy quietly.

'I'm not having trouble taking it in!' said Sonny, his voice breaking embarrassingly into a squeak. 'There's nothing to take in! There's no need to become fans of anything else. Board games, or whatever you were considering.'

'Reptiles?' suggested Jay.

'Bleurgh! No! Not reptiles,' said Sonny angrily. 'There's no need to be fans of anything else. We can still be the Sidekicks! Doctor Extraordinary's coming back – I'm sure of it!'

'OK, OK,' Marcy had said to him soothingly.

But even then he'd known it was no good. Over the following days, every time Sonny had approached them, swinging his bag off his back ready to pull out one of his copies of *Extraordinary Weekly* and discuss it, there'd been those same pitying expressions, as if he'd lost the plot or something. And within a week Marcy and Jay were actively avoiding him.

On the Friday, he'd been just round the corner and overheard them making plans to hang out after school.

'Just the two of us, yeah?' Marcy had said. 'I don't think I can face another speech about, you know, how the doc's going to stage his *incredible reappearance*.'

And, as his two friends laughed, Sonny slunk away.

'I can't say I'm surprised,' said Doctor Extraordinary after listening to this sad tale. 'I've spent the last month wandering round the city, and you're the first person who's really believed I'm still here.'

'To be fair, I *am* the only person who can actually see you' said Sonny, beckoning the ghost back towards the school buildings as the bell for afternoon classes began to ring.

'Well, seeing is believing, as they say,' said the doc thoughtfully. 'But surely you're not the only one who's kept the faith. There must be many people in Paragon

City who long for the return of their hero.'

But sadly Doctor Extraordinary was about to have that fond hope shoved right back in his face like an unwanted spittle-soaked tissue wielded by a chin-wiping grandmother. And it happened during the last lesson of the day, which was Citizenship, when the teacher unfortunately decided to start a moral discussion all about him.

'I really want to do a deep dive into this whole superhero issue,' said Mr Marston. (He constantly tried to get his students to call him by his first name, Johnny, but nobody wanted to.) 'Let's run this up the flagpole and see if it flaps in the breeze, shall we?' He waved his arms, revealing the leather elbow patches on his brown jacket.

'Paragon City used to have a hero to defend it. Now it doesn't. What do we all think about that, guys? And, more importantly, what do we *feel* about it? This is a safe space, right? So, if any of you want to cry, that's cool. Just go with it. Go with the flow. The flow of tears . . . the flow of ideas. Three cheers. You get me?'

The class was looking at him blankly – which was often the case when Mr Marston gave speeches of this kind.

Sonny, who had taken up his usual position in the back row, found his heart sinking even further. He was still attempting to process the fact that the ghost of his hero was sitting invisibly right next to him – the last thing he wanted was a whole-class discussion about him.

'This should be very interesting,' said Doctor Extraordinary, leaning forward keenly.

Sonny wasn't so sure. Who knew what his classmates would say? Already, he noticed glumly, a hand had snapped into the air in front of him.

The arm attached to the hand was clad in a baggy grey jumper with a jagged hole in the elbow. It belonged, Sonny knew, to a girl called Vicky Blott, although nobody ever called her that, using her nickname instead.

'Spot!' said Mr Marston, pointing at her excitedly. 'Yes! What do you have to tell us today?'

There was a buzz of low-level conversation as Spot got to her feet, blowing her unruly dark hair out of her face and removing the very chewed pen that was always clamped between her teeth. She was the smartest student in the class, without a doubt, but she had a dry sense of humour and a knack for saying the wrong thing that tended to keep other people at arm's length. A lot of her classmates made fun of her untidy clothes and the dog-eared notebook that she carried everywhere, and more than once Sonny had been on the cusp of sticking up for her when she'd become the target of cruel jokes.

'Well, sir,' she began, puffing the hair away from her face once again and fiddling with the pen.

'Hey, there's no need to call me sir, Spot,' urged Mr Marston. 'We don't go in for that, like, formal stuff here. I'm not the king! This isn't an episode of, you know, *Branston Abbey* or whatever. Just call me Johnny, OK? Don't know how many times I have to tell you guys.'

Spot coughed in a slightly embarrassed fashion. She had no intention of calling her teacher Johnny. 'I certainly think it's very interesting from a psychological point of view,' she said seriously. 'The way people have fixated on this idealized figure, and the way they're processing his absence in quite a dysfunctional fashion actually.'

There was a silence, broken only by a slight snigger. Mr Marston, who hadn't even begun to understand the previous few sentences, was looking at Spot with his mouth open. It's very frustrating not being as clever as one of your students.

'So sorry . . . wh-wh-what?' he stammered rather lamely. 'But, you know, hero or villain? Was he good for the city, or was he bad for it?'

'Well, *Johnny*,' came a loud voice from the other side of the classroom, 'I think he was a waste of space frankly. I reckon he was pretty cringeworthy. And we're better off without him.'

Spot, with a roll of her eyes, replaced the pen in her mouth as she sat down.

'Who is that child?' a voice hissed from beside Sonny. 'How dare he? That girl sitting in front of us sounded quite clever; this one is downright rude!'

'That's Kyle Lester,' whispered Sonny under his breath. 'Just ignore him. He thinks he's cool.'

But the rest of the class – or a lot of them, at least – seemed to agree with Kyle.

'Yeah, what was with the costume?' someone else piped up. 'It was rubbish!'

'I don't believe it,' muttered Doctor Extraordinary.

'How many times did I save this city? Is that really what people think of me?'

Sonny turned to see that the doc had tears in his eyes.

'I actually always thought Captain Chaos was kind of misunderstood anyway,' said Saoirse Thomas, a lanky girl with dip-dyed blue hair. 'Villains are always the most interesting characters, let's face it.' Sonny heard the doc give a strangled squeak of pure outrage as she went on. 'That whole superhero thing is so last century. It's the sort of thing my dad really likes.' Her lip curled scornfully. 'He always dresses up for the Hero Day Parade and stuff.'

Another voice broke in. 'Oh, my parents do that, too! They've been putting their costumes together ready for the parade next week. Even though we don't even have a hero any more!'

'Right!' someone else piped up. 'I mean, why does the city need some guy in a tight suit to look after it anyway?'

'Don't get me started on that costume,' said Saoirse in disgust. 'I mean, talk about inappropriate.'

Sonny cringed in his chair. He loved the annual Hero Day parade, when thousands of Paragonians paraded through the streets, decked out in home-made superhero outfits. Doctor Extraordinary always did a flypast in his Extra-Jet before handing out prizes for the best-dressed hero during an open-air ceremony in Paragon Park. But this must have been the first time he'd actually had to sit and listen to people criticizing him.

Out of the corner of his eye, Sonny could see the doc listening to the discussion with his mouth and eyes wide open. He looked completely and utterly shell-shocked.

'Don't you think the city's got a bit worse over the last few weeks?' asked Mr Marston, his eyes gleaming at the lively debate he had finally managed to provoke. 'I don't know if you guys have seen the news, but there's been a huge rise in crime and vandalism. The other day, one of the newspapers said Paragon City's turning into a ghost town – people are moving away in their thousands, looking for a better place to live.'

'Well, I still think superheroes are rubbish,' said Saiorse with a snort, and several of her classmates made noises of approval. 'We don't need some idiot in Lycra keeping an eye on us.'

'Yeah,' agreed Kyle. 'We're better off without him. I'm glad he's gone!'

'Shut up,' Sonny blurted loudly, rising to his feet. 'Stop being so mean! Where would the city be without the doc? Remember the bridge at Christmas the other year?'

The whole class had turned to look at him, and he felt his face reddening. Sonny wasn't normally one for big dramatic speeches. But once you've started, it's fairly difficult to stop.

'This is wonderful, Sonny,' said Mr Marston, grinning. 'I'm delighted to see you participating.'

'Even if he is talking a load of rubbish.' Saiorse's blue-tipped hair waggled as she shook her head, and several of her classmates made noises of agreement. 'Someone else would have fixed that bridge. We didn't need a bloke in a tight suit to do it for us.'

'Who would have fixed it?' asked Sonny.

'I dunno – the City Council?' said Saiorse scornfully.

'They can't even collect the bins on the right day!' yelled Sonny. 'Anyway, a bit of gratitude wouldn't hurt, would it? He saved the city over and over again, and here you all are, saying he needn't have bothered. Right in front of him!'

There was a long silence as the whole class stared

at him in confusion. Spot, he could see, had spun right round in her chair and was watching him in fascination, scribbling something in her notebook, which was open on her lap.

'You what?' said Kyle with a sneer. 'What do you mean, right in front of him?'

'He's right here!' Sonny felt like he'd walked right to the end of a diving board, so he might as well jump off. He pointed to Doctor Extraordinary, frozen with shock next to him. 'I think I'm the only one who can see him, though,' he went on a bit lamely.

'Sorry,' said Saiorse Thomas. 'Are you saying that you can see the ghost of Doctor Extraordinary? Right here in this classroom?'

That's weird, thought Sonny, *I didn't think for a split second that she'd actually believe me.*

He nodded enthusiastically, pointing once again to the invisible hero. Then he noticed a mocking smile playing round the corners of the girl's mouth. And the next moment the entire class erupted into a tsunami of laughter. Sonny felt his cheeks flaming and his eyes filling with water as his schoolmates slapped each other on the back and looked at him with expressions of disbelieving delight.

'A ghost!' said Kyle Lester, doubled over and clutching his stomach. 'He thinks he can see a ghost.'

'Not just any ghost, Kyle,' said Saiorse, a wide smile cracking her whole face. 'A *super* ghost!'

The only person not laughing by this point was Spot, who was still staring at Sonny with narrowed eyes and a disconcertingly intense expression behind her curtains of wavy dark hair.

'Calm down, guys, calm down,' said the teacher ineffectually, fanning his hands in a downward gesture. 'Actually, Sonny's method of dealing with his grief is really interesting, and I think we should discuss it as a class. He's actually imagining –'

'I'm not imagining it!' protested Sonny furiously. But it only provoked another wave of hilarity. The laughter washed over him like cold water.

He half turned to look at Doctor Extraordinary, who met his gaze with an expression of horror. The superhero had just experienced the worst ten minutes of his life – sorry, scratch that – the worst ten minutes

of his entire death. He'd spent twenty years protecting this city, and now he had to listen to the people he'd kept safe telling him that, far from being grateful, they actually thought he was a complete has-been, and they were better off without him.

The doc had always had an ear for a dramatic line.

'Nobody believes in me!' wailed the ghost.

CHAPTER 3
THE HAUNTING OF PANDAMONIUM

The baby panda, an adorable bundle of fluffy black-and-white fur, waddled across the floor on its stumpy little legs, uttering a series of incredibly cute squeaking and snuffling noises.

(See, we told you there'd be cute pandas, didn't we?)

'*Squeak, squeak, snuffle,*' went the panda, its huge eyes blinking in the bright light, and its adorable little nose wrinkling curiously. It really was the sweetest, fluffiest thing you'd ever seen. (If we're ever allowed to release merchandise to promote this book, the baby panda will be the number-one bestseller.) Its fur was soft and cuddly; its little pink paws were small and just begged to be tickled.

It was impossible to look at it without going '*Awwww*'.

'*Awwww*,' said everyone in the room. (*Told you*.)

'*Squeak, squeak,* **FZZT**,' said the baby panda, stopping in its tracks and quivering slightly.

'What's going on?' said the woman in the large swivel chair on a raised platform at one end of the room. 'It just went **FZZT**. Pandas don't go **FZZT**.'

She leaned forward, bringing her pale face into the light and revealing that she did not, in fact, look unlike a panda herself. Beneath a mop of jet-black hair, her small eyes were surrounded by wide dark circles.

'**FZZT**,' repeated the baby panda, which was now on the floor in front of her. One of its cute fluffy ears began to emit a thin stream of grey smoke.

'Now it's got smoke coming out of its ear!' protested the woman on the swivel chair. 'That's not right!'

Several men and women in white lab coats were standing along a wall, and one of them stepped forward with an apologetic expression.

'I think there might be a *slight* problem with the robotics,' she said nervously.

At this point, the panda made an even louder '**FZZT**'

noise. Both its eyes popped out on springs and the ear that had been smoking began to belch out a jet of flame.

'A *slight* problem? *Slight?*' squealed the woman. 'Its eyes have gone, and its head's on fire! You call that a *slight* problem? I'd love to see what you think a *big* problem looks like.'

'Erm, like that?' suggested another scientist, pointing to the panda, which had now burst into flames and was crackling merrily like a comforting campfire.

'Get out! Out, out, out! Fix the panda!' said the woman petulantly, rising to her feet and waving her arms in the air. 'I wanted robot panda babies, not walking barbecues!'

The scientists bustled towards the door, one of them grabbing a fire extinguisher and putting out the burning panda before scooping it up into a tub.

'Why does it always have to be pandas anyway?' he mumbled, shaking his scalded fingers.

The woman on the platform glared at him. 'What did you just say?' she asked icily.

'I just said, "Why does it always have to be pandas?"' said the man, shuffling awkwardly as he caught the fury in his boss's gaze.

'It always has to be pandas,' the black-and-white-clothed woman said angrily, 'because I say it's always pandas, because I am PANDAmonium, and I am in charge of this evil empire. Get it?'

'Yes, absolutely,' said the scientist, shoving at his colleagues' backs in his rush to get out of the room.

'The majestic panda is the most enigmatic and powerful animal on the entire planet,' ranted the woman as the last of her staff straggled out of the room. 'I have

chosen to take over the entire world using only panda-based schemes. And I will never be thwarted! The panda is unthwartable! The mightiest and least colourful of all the bears!'

An introduction is probably in order at this point in the book. Who is this strange person and why is she obsessed with pandas? Well, it's an excellent question and thanks for asking it. Her name, as you may have noticed, is PANDAmonium – but you've actually encountered her before, in the prologue. (Oooh, get us, having a prologue! Aren't we fancy! I guess this means that the rest of the book is the 'logue'?)

Anyway, back then, in those far-off prologue days, she was called Anna Podium, and she was Captain Chaos's evil sidekick and chief scientist – remember her on the radio? The bonkers one? Anna Podium had been in charge of building all Captain Chaos's weaponry, which mainly consisted of giant robots of one sort or another. Every villain worth her salt has an evil henchperson of some kind. It's near the top of the villain checklist, in fact. And, if you're wondering what else is on the checklist, here it is in full:

Supervillain Checklist:

1. Evil to the core.
2. Unquenchable thirst for power.
3. Sinister lair, preferably in mountainous setting.
4. Needs an evil sidekick or henchperson (see above).
5. Trademark laugh of some kind – preferably manic.
6. Slightly pointed nose.
7. 'Outie' belly button.
8. Beady eyes.
9. Tea-towel collection.
10. Prefers cats to dogs. (Sorry if this is controversial. We don't make the rules.)

So – to return to item four on the above list – every villain needs an evil sidekick or henchperson. And Captain Chaos's had been Anna Podium. The two women shared many of the same interests – causing chaos, destroying things, plotting attacks on Paragon City and collecting tea towels (see item nine).

Anyway, for many years, Anna had been in most ways an excellent sidekick. She was efficient; she was evil; she was punctual; she was excellent at designing very large and extremely evil robots. But there was one thing about Anna Podium that made her slightly different from your traditional villainous sidekick: she was completely and utterly obsessed with pandas. Each and every item in her tea-towel collection (again, refer to item nine) featured a picture of pandas. Which should have been a clue to her growing madness, to be perfectly honest.

It's hard to say why this bear-based obsession had started, because every time anyone asked Anna about it she gave a different reply. Sometimes she would claim to have been the sole survivor of an aeroplane crash and that she had been raised in the wild by a troupe of pandas.

(This story didn't really add up because she said the crash happened in Finland where there are no wild pandas. In fact, Finland is at least 6,000 kilometres from the nearest wild panda. Plus, the correct word for a group of pandas is not 'a troupe'; it's 'an embarrassment of pandas' or 'a cupboard of pandas'. (Seriously, we just looked it up.))

At other times, Anna Podium would tell people that she'd grown up at the family zoo, where a kindly old panda couple had adopted her while her real parents were busy feeding the zebras. She'd also maintained that she'd been bitten by a radioactive panda, that one of her grandparents was actually a panda, or that pandas are in fact the dominant species on Planet Earth and are responsible for all modern inventions, including denim, the internal combustion engine, and shoes.

None of this was true, of course – as far as we know, at least. She was just a strange little woman who really, really liked pandas. But it made her slightly irritating as a sidekick because she was always trying to insert pandas into any evil scheme Captain Chaos came up with. Take, for example, what happened a few months before this book started . . .

Wearing her trademark multicoloured outfit, Captain Chaos strode into her supervillain control room where her faithful sidekick was waiting for her.

'Morning, Anna,' she said evilly. 'I was thinking it was about time we plotted another dastardly attack on Paragon City.'

Anna Podium's dark-ringed eyes lit up. 'Splendid idea!' she said greedily. 'I think I have just the thing.'

'Well, technically,' Captain Chaos corrected her, 'as the supervillain, it will be me who comes up with the evil plan. And your job, as sidekick, is to rub your hands together, chuckle in an evil fashion and congratulate me on the splendid, erm, evillity, of my evil plan. OK?'

Anna bridled a little at this. 'Well, yes,' she said, 'but I really think you might want to listen to my evil plan first. It really is very, very evil.'

Captain Chaos sighed slightly. 'It's pandas, isn't it?'

'What?' The other woman looked at her suspiciously.

'Is your plan,' the captain went on, 'panda-based in some way?'

'Well . . .' Anna Podium waved her hands. 'There is a pandarous element to it, yes. But I wouldn't go so far as to call it panda-based.'

'Panda-inspired, then?' asked Captain Chaos. 'Panda-centric?'

'Tinged with pandarosity, I would say,' suggested her sidekick.

'In that case, no, I don't want to hear it,' said Captain Chaos firmly. 'As I've told you, I don't intend to use pandas in any of my evil plans. Perhaps one day, if you become a supervillain yourself, you can do all your panda plots. But, until then, you're the sidekick, and I'll be the one hatching the schemes, OK?'

Well, just you wait and see, Anna thought to herself. *One day I'll be in charge of this evil operation. And, when I am, it's going to be pandas a gogo.*

Outwardly, she gave an oily, sidekicky grin and asked, 'So what is your evil plan, Captain?'

'Robots,' said Captain Chaos, smiling. 'Giant robots.'

'How original,' said Anna with a sneer, but not loudly enough for her boss to hear.

It has been said before, and rightly so, that there's a major problem with villainous sidekicks. And the problem is that they're always plotting against you. Anna Podium, as well as being completely obsessed with pandas, was also extremely clever, entirely ruthless and completely and utterly cuckoo-clock unhinged in the head, which is a really awkward combination to have in one of your employees.

Captain Chaos realized this slightly too late – shortly before her giant robot exploded with her inside it. And, as that happened, Anna Podium had rubbed her hands together in triumph. Finally, her time had come. She immediately gathered the staff at Castle Chaos together and made a couple of announcements:

Announcement 1: She was now assuming control of the entire Chaos operation. From henceforth, she would be in charge. And all future evil plots would be, without exception, entirely panda-based.

Announcement 2: She was changing her name. Anna Podium is a reasonable enough name for a scientist, but it's not really evil enough for a supervillain. So, with immediate effect, the leader of the Chaos operation would be known as PANDAmonium. (She tried out 'Anna-panda-podium', but it was a little too silly for her.) Which is a shame because it made us laugh a lot.

*

And that brings us back to the woman now known as PANDAmonium, sitting alone in the supervillain control room, having chased all her scientists away to continue work on the robot baby pandas. She gnawed at a fingernail in frustration, spinning the chair round and round.

'Why can't they get it right?' she muttered to herself furiously. 'Why can't they build a working baby panda robot?'

A large amount of baby pandas were essential to her plan – they would provide a vital distraction while she put her main plot into operation. A plot that was also, if you needed reminding, based round a certain black-and-white bear.

As PANDAmonium spun round and round in the chair, a bright flash of colour met her eyes. She was going too fast to see exactly what it was, so she waited for the chair to slow down slightly. As she made another revolution, she scuffed her feet on the floor to bring the chair to a complete stop, widening her eyes in shock. There, at the back of the control room, with her arms folded and an angry expression on her face, was Captain Chaos.

105

PANDAmonium's brain reeled. Her mouth opened and closed, but no recognizable sounds came out of it. (We'll write them down anyway, just to help set the scene, but we just wanted to give you prior warning that they don't make any sense.)

'**FLEEERGH**,' said PANDAmonium. '**BEP. AFLARGHA. BEMBLE. PEP? FLEFF. WHOOT**.'

'What on earth are you blithering about?' said Captain Chaos, frowning.

'**WHAAGH!**' PANDAmonium started up from the chair in surprise. 'It really is you! I thought you were . . . you know. One of those things that you think is there, but then it isn't really there.'

'A hallucination?'

'A pigeon!' blurted PANDAmonium. 'I looked out of the window the other day and saw a pigeon, then when I looked back a bit later it had completely disappeared!'

'Well, it had probably flown away,' said Captain Chaos reasonably.

'Oh yes.' Her sidekick furrowed her brow. 'I hadn't thought of that.'

'Look, this isn't relevant!' snapped Captain Chaos.

'Why are you dribbling on about pigeons when there's an actual ghost standing in the room, talking to you?'

'A ghost?' PANDAmonium's face drained of colour.

'Well, what else would you call me?' asked the late supervillain. 'And if you say pigeon,' she added, 'I shall scream.'

PANDAmonium had very mixed feelings about what she was currently seeing. Mainly, she was confused and terrified. But she was also slightly miffed. She'd been very much enjoying running the supervillain operation herself, barking at scientists and – finally – plotting evil panda plans. The sudden reappearance of her boss would have been fairly horrifying, even if the boss in question hadn't been dead.

'B-but . . . how?' she stammered.

Captain Chaos had been considering this very question herself. 'We can work that out later,' she said curtly. 'Firstly, I want to know what's been going on here. What on earth do you think you're doing? What was all that with the robot panda? What have you done with my lovely supervillain operation? I told you specifically: *no pandas*.'

'Well –' a sly smirk appeared on PANDAmonium's

face – 'that was when you were in charge. Now I'm the supervillain, I can have as many pandas as I want.'

'And how many pandas do you want?'

'Lots.' PANDAmonium's dark eyes gleamed. 'Thousands and thousands of them.'

CHAPTER 4
DO YOU BELIEVE IN GHOSTS?

Doctor Extraordinary left school that day in an extremely sombre mood. He was so far down in the dumps that Sonny decided he needed to set aside his anger at being abandoned by his hero. It was time to actually enjoy being the only person in the world who could see the doc. And he also hoped that by behaving a bit more like a proper number-one fan it might cheer the mopey ghost up a bit.

'Come in, come in,' he said, beckoning the doc into his bedroom. 'Have a look at all these posters. Here's one of the Extra-Jet – look!'

Doctor Extraordinary regarded it morosely, his

black-gloved hands hanging miserably by his sides.

'Who are you talking to?' asked his dad from the living room.

'Just the cat!' said Sonny airily. 'I'm, er . . . showing him some of my posters.'

He heard his dad mumble something in reply that may or may not have contained the words 'cat', 'talking' and 'completely crackers'.

Sonny swung his rucksack off his back and tipped the contents out on to the bed. Along with a few schoolbooks and a pencil case, the bag was completely stuffed with copies of *Extraordinary Weekly*, the doc's official fan-club magazine.

'I've got loads of questions,' said Sonny excitedly, kicking the door shut so his dad wouldn't overhear any more and think he was now interviewing the cat. 'To start with, I want to know all about the first time I ever saw you in action . . . What are you looking at?'

Doctor Extraordinary had wandered over to the window and now stood gazing gloomily out across the city. 'How can they say they don't need me?' he said softly, almost to himself. 'I've defended this city for twenty years.'

Sonny decided that now wasn't the time to ask the doc to relive some of his exploits. Even though he was bursting with questions, perhaps a slight period of adjustment was going to be needed before he got all the backstage gossip. After all, Sonny reasoned to himself, looking sadly at Doctor Extraordinary's forlorn, droop-shouldered posture, it wasn't every day that the ghost of a superhero had to listen to a whole class of schoolkids saying they thought superheroes were completely overrated.

And so Sonny settled in to spend a nice, calm evening with the ghost of his hero. Which is just as odd an experience as that sentence makes it sound. Having a ghost living with you is not unlike owning a pet dog. They follow you around all over the place; they constantly want your attention, but they're unable to help with the washing-up – or any household chores, for that matter. And, unlike a dog, they can also walk through walls, which can be very awkward if you're in the bath. Basically, to put it in a nutshell, you never get a moment's peace.

'Looks like fajitas for tea,' said Doctor Extraordinary a little later, striding through Sonny's bedroom door without opening it. He had cheered up slightly after spending half an hour brooding. 'I've been doing a bit of exploring, spying out the lie of the land, you know. Your dad's just started cooking. I had a nice sit-down in the bathroom for a while, too. But I had to get out when he walked in on me.'

'Thank goodness for that,' said Sonny, deciding he did not want to hear another word of that particular anecdote.

Doctor Extraordinary behaved himself throughout the evening, sitting quietly while Sonny had tea and did his homework. But when it was time for bed things got slightly awkward.

'What do you think you're doing?' said Sonny, coming back into the room in his pyjamas and wiping toothpaste from around his mouth. The doc had settled himself on a comfy chair in the corner of his bedroom.

'What do you mean?'

'Well, you can't just sit there while I go to sleep!'

'Why ever not?'

'Are you serious?' Sonny stood by his bed, one foot ready to plunge under the duvet. 'You really think I'm

going to settle down for the night with an actual ghost sitting in the corner of my bedroom, staring at me?'

'Well, what do you expect me to do?' asked Doctor Extraordinary. 'I don't go to sleep myself. In fact, I don't really do anything. I *can't* do anything!' He thought about this for a moment. 'Actually, it's rather boring being a ghost. I haven't had a proper conversation with anyone for a month.'

'Well, that's very sad,' said Sonny, 'but I still can't have you sitting quietly in the corner while I sleep. It's creepy!'

'Well, can I put the TV on, then?'

'Of course you can't put the TV on! How would I get to sleep?'

'I'll wear headphones. Oh no, hang on. I can't wear headphones. I don't have a real head. Well, shall

I go and sit in your dad's room?'

'What? No!' Sonny sat down on the edge of the bed.

'Why not? He can't even see me!'

'And you think that makes it less creepy?' Sonny sighed. 'OK then,' he relented. 'You can stay in here. Just don't, you know, look at me. Turn the chair round or something.'

'I can't turn the chair round!'

'Oh, honestly!'

Huffily, Sonny stomped over and turned the chair round to face the window.

'There,' he said. 'Just sit here quietly, OK?'

'Don't worry,' said the ghost. 'You won't even know I'm here.'

'That's definitely one of the top three creepiest things a ghost in your bedroom could possibly say,' replied Sonny. 'Just below "sweet dreams".'

'And what's the creepiest thing a ghost in your bedroom could possibly say?' enquired our hero.

'Well, "Boo!" obviously,' said Sonny matter-of-factly. 'Now keep quiet. See you in the morning.'

'Sweet dreams,' said Doctor Extraordinary. 'Oh sorry. Creepy. Goodnight.'

'Night,' said Sonny, turning over and switching off his bedside light.

As Sonny walked to school the following morning, he heard running footsteps behind him.

'Who are you talking to?' said a voice, panting.

He turned to see Vicky Blott rushing to catch up with him, pen clamped between her teeth and notebook in hand as usual.

'I've decided to study you,' she announced ominously as she skidded to a halt beside him, her baggy grey jumper flapping in the morning breeze. 'Your delusion is a very common side effect of grief, you know. I had a flick

through some of my mum's old psychology textbooks last night.'

'Morning, Spot,' said Sonny, feeling slightly flattered that at least someone was taking an interest in him, even if it was the rather forbiddingly brainy class science nerd.

'So,' said Spot, falling into step beside him and snapping off the elastic band that held her notebook shut, 'to return to my question: who were you talking to? Were you, in your grief-stricken state, actually holding an imaginary conversation with Doctor Extraordinary? It's fine to say,' she added, swishing her dark hair casually. 'I'm a professional. Well, I've read all the books, at least.'

'No, I was not having an imaginary conversation with Doctor Extraordinary,' Sonny told her quite truthfully.

He had, in fact, been chatting to the doc, who had insisted on coming to school with him again after distracting him all through breakfast by pretending to ride the dog round the flat. Sonny had been unable to explain to his dad why he'd suddenly found the dog so funny.

'You weren't talking to his ghost, then?' persisted Spot, puffing at her hair so she could shoot him a keen, searching glance.

'Well –' Sonny looked sideways at her – 'would you actually believe me if I told you I was?'

'No,' she replied frankly, pausing in her stride to jot something down in her notebook. 'There is no scientific basis for the existence of ghosts. And one should never theorize without data, as I'm sure you know.'

'Well, I can see him, right there,' said Sonny stubbornly, pointing to what was – to Spot – an empty patch of pavement beside them. 'Doesn't that count as data?'

Spot stopped walking and peered at Sonny, legs crossed and eyes narrowed. 'Not really, no,' she said slowly. 'Sorry.'

'How rude!' exclaimed Doctor Extraordinary. 'I think the evidence of your own eyes is perfectly good data.'

'He says that was very rude,' said Sonny. 'And that the evidence of my own eyes is perfectly good data. So there,' he added, giving her a slight smile.

It felt nice to be chatting to a real-live person, even if she did think he was completely deluded. Since he'd fallen out with the other Sidekicks, Sonny's schooldays had mostly been chat-free.

Spot was still looking at him keenly. 'Are you actually serious?' she asked, blowing her hair out of her face once again. 'Do you actually expect me to believe you can see the ghost of Doctor Extraordinary?'

'I don't expect you to believe it,' said Sonny honestly, 'but I wish someone would. He's literally standing right next to you.'

Spot looked uncertainly to her left.

'No, the other side,' said Sonny, and she looked the other way, squinting down the street, which was completely empty apart from a few hurrying schoolkids.

'Come on,' she told him after a moment, snapping the notebook closed. 'We can finish this talk later. If we don't run, we're going to be late, Ghost Boy.'

Together they rushed down the road and in through the school gates. Sonny's heart sank as they pushed through the doors and into the hallway. Kyle Lester was lounging against a wall, surrounded by a group of his friends.

'Whoo! Look out, everyone!' he said mockingly when he caught sight of Sonny. 'The school is now officially haunted!' He held out his hands in front of him and wiggled his fingers while widening his eyes. 'The *ghooooooost* of Doctor Extraordinary is here!'

'Really,' said Doctor Extraordinary dismissively. 'That child is very irritating.'

'Just ignore him,' said Sonny, putting his head down and marching past.

'He's talking to himself!' said one of Kyle's friends.

'I'm not, actually,' said Sonny tensely.

'Who are you talking to, then?' asked Kyle, leaning forward in mock interest. 'The ghost?'

'Yes, in fact I am,' said Sonny. 'Now please get out of my way.'

The whole crowd dissolved into fresh howls of laughter as he pushed past.

'He's not going to let this go, is he?' Sonny said in frustration as he hurried away down the corridor. 'I just wish I knew something I could use to shut him up. Like an embarrassing secret or something.'

'Well,' said Spot, who had kept pace with him, 'let's treat this scientifically.'

'Do you always treat everything scientifically?' asked Sonny.

'Yes, of course,' Spot replied. 'This could be very helpful

in dispelling your delusion. Scientifically speaking, if you really did know a ghost, surely they'd be able to snoop around and find out something embarrassing about Kyle Lester. So, when you discover that's not physically possible, maybe you'll realize . . .'

But she trailed off when she noticed that Sonny had stopped in his tracks and was staring at her with an expression of dawning delight.

'Brilliant, Spot!' he said. 'That's totally brilliant! You're right! The doc can ghost his way into Kyle's house and find out something embarrassing about him! And then maybe you'll believe me, too!'

'That wasn't actually my very scientific plan,' Spot told him, frowning in disapproval. 'I was simply thinking that, if you discovered your ghost can't really find out a secret, your brain would be forced to accept that you'd imagined the whole thing.'

'Yeah, I get that,' said Sonny, grinning widely at her. 'But if the doc *does* discover something, something nobody else could possibly find out, you know what I'd call that?'

'Erm . . .' Spot looked confused. 'No, what?'

'Well, Spot,' said Sonny slyly, exchanging a wink with Doctor Extraordinary. 'I think I'd call it data.'

That night, Sonny was waiting down the road from Kyle Lester's house when Doctor Extraordinary came racing round the corner, wearing a triumphant expression.

'Did you get something?' Sonny asked breathlessly.

'Oh, indeed I did,' said the doc excitedly. 'Not only does Kyle Lester go to bed in pink elephant pyjamas, but he refuses to go to sleep unless his mum has tucked him in with his favourite teddy, whose name is Paul W. Bear.'

'*Yesssss!*' Sonny punched the air in delight.

The following morning, Sonny walked into school with a much more confident air. Spot was waiting for him in the playground, arms crossed, with an expression that said, *I'm about to be proved right, as usual.* She squealed in shock when Sonny, beaming, grabbed her by the elbow and dragged her along with him.

'Check out this data,' he told her proudly as they burst through the front doors. As expected, Kyle Lester and his hangers-on were waiting for him in the entrance hall.

'Ghost Boy is here!' wailed Kyle in a mocking tone. 'Look out, everyone – we're being haunted!'

'Don't be scared, Kyle,' Sonny shot back. 'If you get a bit spooked, you can always cuddle Paul W. Bear.'

'Wh-wh-what?' stammered Kyle, a flush of deep red shooting up his face. 'Dunno what you're talking about!'

'Oh, you know Paul, don't you?' said Sonny, advancing on him. 'Your little bedtime pal? Your mum tucks you up with Paul every night, doesn't she? Just after you put on your pink elephant pyjamas?'

By now, Kyle was backing away from him, his face crimson and his eyes wide.

'Have you been spying on me, you freak?' he said, horrified.

His friends looked at him in amused horror – he'd just admitted that Sonny was telling the truth.

'You don't really have pink elephant pyjamas, do you?' said one of them.

'And a teddy?' asked another.

'Shut up!' snapped Kyle. Abruptly, he pushed through his crowd of cronies and disappeared down the hallway as they giggled and pointed after him.

Sonny turned to Spot, his face flushed with triumph. 'Data,' he told her proudly. 'Nobody except the ghost could have found that out.'

'Scientifically speaking, that's completely and utterly wrong,' said Spot, pulling her pen out of her mouth and opening her notebook. She jotted down a few lines. 'But your case continues to interest me. I'm willing to suggest a temporary arrangement so I can gather more information.'

'Oh yes?'

'Yes. I'm proposing that we spend some time in each other's company so I can study your claims about this supposed ghost.'

'So you want to hang out together?' asked Sonny, suddenly feeling slightly shy. 'Be friends?'

'No!' said Spot in horror, her mop of hair falling in front of her face. 'Friendship is highly unscientific. It's a temporary arrangement where we, you know, talk.'

'Get doughnuts?' suggested Sonny.

'It's possible,' Spot agreed.

'Have lunch together at school?'

'That sounds like a potentially valuable data exchange, yes.'

'You help me with my science homework?'

'Certainly not!'

'Fine.' Sonny Nelson held out a hand. 'But I can't wait for the day you have to admit you were wrong. Doctor Extraordinary is standing right next to you.'

'Scientists never admit they were wrong,' said Spot with a sniff.

Up the mountain, inside the thick walls of Castle Chaos, ghost/human relations were not quite so rosy.

'I'm in control of this evil operation!' insisted Captain Chaos, stamping her invisible foot and making no sound at all. 'It's my castle! Those are my scientists! And I'm the one who comes up with all the evil plots!'

'Ah,' said PANDAmonium, raising an infuriating finger, 'but nobody can see you apart from me, can they? How are you expecting to run your evil empire without my help?'

Captain Chaos thought about this for a moment. Annoyingly, her second in command was absolutely right. The captain had spent some time wandering round Paragon City and her own castle, attempting to talk to people, but nobody apart from PANDAmonium could see or hear her. This was frustrating, as the thought of being an evil ghost was extremely attractive to her.

When she'd first discovered that she was still, somehow, present after the explosion, she had hatched several evil plots involving haunting people or knocking things over. But you can't haunt people if they can't see you, and you can't knock things over if your hand simply slides through them. She had wasted several days in a lonely house on a nearby hillside trying to frighten the family that lived there, before reluctantly admitting to herself that they were unhauntable. She was just a strange, invisible woman going 'Boo!' in wardrobes with no practical results whatsoever.

When the captain had realized that PANDAmonium could see her, she'd been excited. *Finally*, she had thought, *a chance to get my evil operation up and running again.* But her deputy had other ideas. She'd been very much enjoying being in charge for a change, and was reluctant to hand back the reins of power. Not without doing a bit of bargaining first, anyway.

'Look,' said PANDAmonium reasonably, settling herself on the large, padded swivel chair. 'I'm sure we can work this out.'

'That's my chair,' said Captain Chaos irritably. 'That's the main baddie chair – you know that. I sit there.'

She had spent a great deal of time and expense a few years back designing this chair and having it built to her own specifications. It was very large, upholstered in jet-black leather with the letters CC embossed on the oversized backrest.

She pointed. 'It's even got my initials on it.'

'But you're a ghost,' said PANDAmonium with a small smile. 'And your life – or your death, rather – has changed a bit. The good news is you can walk through walls. The bad news is you can't sit on a chair. Not even one with your own initials on. In fact, I might even change the chair – put my own initials on it instead.'

Captain Chaos was stung. 'You most certainly will not!' she said furiously. 'What do you mean by your initials anyway? You've only got one. What are you going to do? Put a big P on the back?'

'I'll make it say P-N-D-M-N-M,' said PNDmnm smugly, reaching up and running a hand over the leather behind her head.

'But, but . . .' Captain Chaos sputtered, 'those aren't initials! That's just your name with the vowels taken out!'

'So?' PANDAmonium shrugged. 'It's cool. And I'm the lady with the bad-girl chair. I can do what I like.'

'That does it,' snapped Captain Chaos. With a dive, she launched herself on to the chair and attempted to sit down.

'Get off me!' said PANDAmonium, wriggling as the ghost assumed a sitting position right on top of, and in many ways through, her. 'Look, this bickering is pointless. You're being a T-T-L L-M-N.'

'I understood that, and I am not a total lemon!' protested the captain. 'All right, then,' she conceded, stepping back. 'You can sit in the chair for now. But only because I can't. On the condition that you help me formulate a new evil plan to destroy Paragon City.'

'Oh yes,' said PANDAmonium, smirking. 'I have some very, very evil ideas – don't you worry.'

'Let me guess,' Captain Chaos replied. 'Do they involve pandas at all?'

'No,' mumbled PANDAmonium, looking slightly awkward.

In fact, her plan involved literally thousands of pandas, but she'd been offended by Captain Chaos implying that pandas were all she ever thought about. Even though it was plainly true. Absolutely everything in her life was panda-themed, and we're not just talking about her duvet cover. Her bed was panda-shaped. Her toothbrush was whittled into the form of a panda. She'd even made her scientific team spend three weeks designing a special toaster that scorched a panda face into each slice of bread, and she refused to eat anything that didn't use these bear-blazoned slices to make what she insisted on calling pand-wiches.

'Definitely not?' asked the captain suspiciously.

'Absolutely not.'

There was a short pause.

'Well,' PANDAmonium continued, 'there is a small chance that pandas are involved somewhere along the line. But only in a limited way.'

Captain Chaos gave a small sigh. 'Go on, then.'

'Right.' PANDAmonium rubbed her hands together, leaning forward excitedly in the chair that wasn't hers. 'Here's the plan. Phase One: we send small, cute robot pandas into Paragon City – thousands of them. I've had my scientific team – sorry, *your* scientific team – designing them for weeks now, and they're nearly ready.'

'And what is the purpose of sending a load of cute robot pandas into the city?'

'Well, for a start, the city will be full of pandas,' said PANDAmonium, as if that was reason enough. 'But then comes the really, really evil part. Once we are ready, we activate Phase Two of the plan. On my command – sorry, on your command – all the robot pandas will turn evil. And that's when you launch your main attack, and you'll like this! It shall be carried out in your very favourite way – by using a giant robot! But this time there's a twist!'

'Is it a giant robot panda?' asked Captain Chaos, slightly wearily.

'It's a giant robot panda!' PANDAmonium shrieked in delight, pretending she hadn't heard. 'A giant panda, but a GIANT one. A GIANT giant panda. A GIANT robotic giant panda.'

'I thought you said this plan involved pandas in a limited way?' said Captain Chaos.

'Yes,' said PANDAmonium quizzically. 'Why do you ask?'

'Well, it's just that this plan is entirely panda-centric. There is no small detail of this whole scheme,' pointed out Captain Chaos, 'that is not entirely centred round the panda.'

'You're a ghost,' retorted PANDAmonium, 'so, really, what are you going to do about it? You can't even sit in your own chair. If you want to attack the city, you're going to have to use one of my ideas for once. It's the panda way or the highway.'

Captain Chaos sighed. 'Fine. Whatever. Show me these robot pandas, then.'

'Excellent!' shouted PANDAmonium, getting up from the chair with a cackle of evil laughter. 'Prepare to be bamboozled! That's a pun on the word "bamboo", which is a panda's favourite food,' she explained, as she led the way out of the control room.

'It's not really a great evil catchphrase if you have to explain it,' muttered Captain Chaos as she followed.

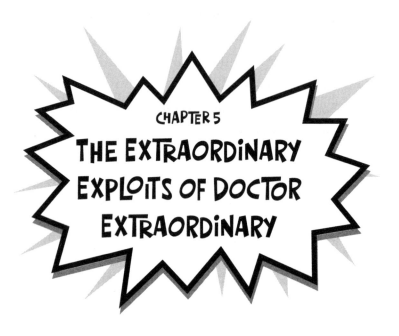

CHAPTER 5

THE EXTRAORDiNARY EXPLOiTS OF DOCTOR EXTRAORDiNARY

It's surprisingly difficult to have a proper conversation with a ghost. Sonny was absolutely desperate to pick Doctor Extraordinary's brains for juicy behind-the-scenes superhero secrets, but every time he did so he was interrupted by his dad shouting, 'Who are you talking to?'

Even on the way to and from school, it was hard to hold a conversation without looking like he was sitting on the Loop talking loudly to himself. Eventually, Sonny decided that the only way to get some proper alone time with his ghostly hero was to be – well – alone. And, with that in mind, the following Saturday he took the doc to the edge of Lake Sunrise.

It was a warm, sunny day, and the lakefront was filled with people strolling, eating ice creams and gazing out across the calm water. Sonny made his way through the crowds towards the small beach where a brightly painted stand rented out pedal boats.

'Just for you, is it?' said the sulky-looking teenager running the stall. He eyed Sonny critically, the wispy moustache on his upper lip fluttering in a slight breeze from the lake. 'Most people don't take pedaloes out on their own. If you're on your own, you want a kayak, don't you?'

'I don't want a kayak, thanks,' said Sonny firmly. 'One pedalo, please. For one.'

'Have it your way,' said the youth with a sigh, and he held a smart red pedal boat still while Sonny clambered across into the right-hand seat.

'He's rather rude, isn't he?' said Doctor Extraordinary, climbing aboard invisibly. 'If I wasn't a ghost, I'd push him in.' He mimed a shoving motion towards the youth, sticking out his tongue.

Sonny broke into a laugh, which caused the moody young boatman to frown at him.

'Be back in an hour,' he said, shoving the boat away from the shore with his grubby trainer. Sonny waved at him cheerily, and began to pedal, aiming to get as far away as possible so he could chat to the ghost of his hero undisturbed.

'I wish you could help with the pedalling,' he said a few minutes later when his T-shirt was stuck to his back with sweat. It was hard work propelling the boat all on his own, and, with only the right-hand set of pedals being used, it kept veering to the left.

'I'd pedal if I could, promise,' said the doc airily.

He was looking out into the distance with his hands behind his head, enjoying the sunny weather. Sonny shot him a dark look. Eventually, they were far enough away from everyone else for Sonny to stop the boat and turn to Doctor Extraordinary as the pedalo bobbed placidly on the clear water.

'Right,' he said, 'finally, nobody to ask who I'm talking to.'

'I'm at your service,' said the doc. 'Fire away. My

mission, should I choose to accept it – which I do – is to answer any and all questions you may have pertaining to my superhero career with the truth, the whole truth and nothing but the truth. What do you want to know?'

Sonny felt slightly floored by this question. What did he want to know? It's not every day you get to interview your greatest hero.

'Basically,' he told Doctor Extraordinary, 'I want to know everything. But we've only got an hour before we have to return the boat to that rude guy. So let's start with the day you stopped that bank robbery.'

It was a day Sonny Nelson remembered with perfect clarity. It was the very first time he had seen the doc in action. The day he'd become a fan. It had been early on Sunday morning around five years ago, and Sonny and his dad had headed out early to their favourite doughnut shop, which was called Go Nuts for Doughnuts. They had one particular speciality – the Double Custard Paragon Paradise, which Officer Dusty Nelson treated his son to when he'd done something especially noteworthy.

Having brought some good test results home from

school, Sonny was in line for a DCPP, as everyone called them, and his mouth was watering as they walked down the almost deserted street towards the cafe, chatting about this and that as they always used to. They'd just been laughing about how many doughnuts they'd eat, Sonny recalled, with a sudden pang of regret for the fun they used to have together before he'd become Doctor Extraordinary's number-one fan rather than his dad's.

'That's funny,' Officer Dusty had said as they passed a large stone-clad building with a sign declaring it to be the headquarters of Paragon Savings and Loans. 'Surely there shouldn't be any lights on in the bank on a Sunday?'

They had stopped on the corner, and Sonny peered down a dingy alley beside the office block.

'There's a van parked down there, Dad,' he said. 'Look!'

As they did so, a man darted from the grubby white van and into a side door of the building.

'I don't like this,' said Officer Dusty. He reached towards his belt for his radio. 'I'd better call it in.'

But before he could act there was a deep rumbling sound, and the entire building began to shake. With a

tearing noise and a shower of concrete chips, the bank rose slowly off the ground. As the dust settled, a figure was visible behind it, holding the building up in the air as if it weighed next to nothing.

'Morning, officer!' called Doctor Extraordinary brightly. 'No need for any action from you. I have the situation under control. If you're on your way for breakfast, I suggest Go Nuts for Doughnuts. Do you know it?' Officer Dusty nodded dumbly, staring with his mouth open.

'There's someone inside there!' said Sonny, who in his excitement had been unable to say anything for the past few seconds. 'At least one person!'

He'd been aware of the superhero, of course. Everybody in Paragon City knew that the doc swooped in whenever liberty was threatened and all that. But this was the first time Sonny had actually witnessed some actual, live, in-person swoopage.

'Ah yes,' said our hero, 'very good point. I think it's time I made a withdrawal from this particular bank, don't you? And deposit these wrongdoers in prison. Deposit, get it?' he added over his shoulder as he turned, hefting the huge building in his hands. 'First of all, though, let's make sure they don't get any ideas about running away.'

Balancing the bank on one finger like a basketball, he spun it round several times with his other hand.

'That should make them nicely dizzy,' he said to Officer Dusty conversationally. 'So your colleagues at the police station won't have any trouble with them. Well, good day to you.'

And, with that, he walked casually away down the

street, still carrying the bank above his head.

Back on the pedalo, Doctor Extraordinary smiled sadly. 'Ah yes, I remember it well,' said the doc. 'So you were the little chap on his way to get doughnuts, were you? How incredible.'

'And ever since that day I've been your biggest fan,' Sonny told him proudly.

And that's probably understandable, to be fair. It's not every day you see someone spinning an entire bank round on their finger like a pizza.

'So,' Sonny said excitedly, 'tell me about some more of your adventures.'

'Well.' The doc closed his eyes for a second in thought. 'What about the time that factory was on fire? That was fairly dramatic.'

'Yes, that sounds like a good one,' said Sonny.

'So this factory was ablaze, and I rushed to the scene. I immediately realized that I needed to extinguish the flames. So I simply picked up the entire factory, brought it here to the lake and dipped it in. Then I carried it back and replaced it.'

'Right,' said Sonny. 'So is it mainly carrying buildings about, then?'

'Not at all,' retorted the doc. 'I do lots of things! Carrying buildings about is just, ah, a small part of it. I do recall I said something quite witty, though, while I was moving the factory.'

He smirked as he remembered his own quip.

'It was a clothing factory, you see, and, as I carried it towards the lake, I said, "Seems like these really *are* the hottest looks this season."' He laughed out loud. 'The factory was on fire, you see,' he explained, apparently puzzled that Sonny wasn't in complete hysterics. 'So it was extremely hot.'

'Oh yes, very good,' said Sonny with a polite smile as he pedalled the boat round a red-and-white-striped buoy.

'And what about the day the bridge collapsed?' the doc went on quickly, keen to regain some momentum after his 'hottest looks' quip had fallen so flat. 'Remember? On Christmas Eve?'

'Oh yes!'

Sonny did indeed remember that day from a couple of years before. He and his dad had been due to drive out

140

of the city to visit his grandma a few hours away, when the news had come on the radio that the main bridge out of town had collapsed. But Doctor Extraordinary had saved the day once again. He had lifted the two halves of the bridge back into place and held them there for the whole of Christmas Eve and Christmas Day, only pausing briefly on Boxing Day to eat some turkey sandwiches. And, what's more, he'd entertained passing motorists with a selection of carols and festive songs as the cars had streamed in and out of Paragon City on their festive visits.

'The day I saved Christmas,' said Doctor Extraordinary nostalgically and not at all modestly, after he'd told Sonny the story.

'What else, what else?' said Sonny eagerly, glancing at his watch.

Time was running out. And, as much as he could spend all day listening to dramatic rescue missions, he realized there was one story he really, really wanted to hear. A story that only the man sitting with him in the pedalo could really tell.

'Tell me about the day you became a hero,' begged

Sonny Nelson. 'What really happened?'

'Well that,' said Doctor Extraordinary, 'is perhaps the most extraordinary story of all.'

And, as the sunlight caught the ripples of Lake Sunrise, and the chatter of the crowd reached them from the distant shore, he told Sonny Nelson about the day that life in Paragon City changed for everybody.

'Of course, back then,' he said, 'my name wasn't Doctor Extraordinary. Back then, I was plain old Doctor Xavier Arden . . .'

If this was a film, at this point the screen would go all fuzzy and harp music would tinkle. But, as it's a book, you'll have to replicate this effect by squinting your eyes slightly and making harp-esque noises with your mouth. Ready?

BLUBLUBLUBLBUBLUB BRRRRRRiiiiiNNNNGGGGG.
PLiNG PLiNG PLiNG PLiNG PLiNK.
STRUUUMMMMMMMM.

(Harp noises are hard to write down.)

'Do keep up, Case!' snapped Doctor Xavier Arden, the

world's most eminent authority on meteorites, as he toiled up a narrow mountain path. His assistant, Catherine Case, had stopped a little way back down the track to sniff some wild flowers.

('We were on our way to investigate reports of a very mysterious meteorite,' explained Doctor Extraordinary back in the pedalo.

'Aren't all meteorites mysterious?' asked Sonny. 'You know, what with coming from space and all.'

'Well, yes, technically that's true,' admitted the doc, 'but stop asking questions. You're interrupting the flashback.'

'Sorry,' said Sonny.)

Back in the past, Doctor Xavier – or Doctor X as he was known to the scientific community – looked down at the map clutched in his hands. 'Nearly there now, Case,' he said sternly. 'Do try and focus this time.'

Catherine Case abandoned her flower-sniffing and ambled up the path to join him. In contrast to Doctor X with his smart suit, she was dressed in brightly coloured and mismatched clothing.

'Come on, then,' she said to him, breaking into a jog. 'Last one to touch the meteorite is a mouldy sausage.'

Doctor Xavier's eyebrows shot up. 'We will certainly

not be running up to the meteorite and touching it,' he told her sternly.

He pulled a large, thick book out of his overcoat pocket and brandished it, pointing at the title: *Meteorite Investigation: Rules, Procedures and Techniques.*

'We shall be carefully following –' he stabbed at each word with a finger – 'the rules, the procedures and the techniques. Substances from space can be extremely dangerous. There may be elements inside this meteorite completely unknown to humanity. Who knows what they may be, or what effect they might have on the unwary or the incautious?'

'Oh, lighten up,' said Catherine Case.

As she spoke, they reached the brow of the hill. Spread before them was a large smoking crater in the mountainside. At the bottom of it, a purplish-coloured circular rock was sticking out of a ridge in the soil, emitting a strange other-worldly light.

'Cool, it's a glowing one!' said Catherine in wonder, starting off down the hill. 'Let's get down there and have a poke about!'

'Have a poke about?' Doctor Xavier Arden followed

his assistant, waving his rule book furiously. 'Serious scientists do not "have a poke about",' he continued snootily. 'Do you think the geniuses who split the atom were just "having a poke about"?'

'Well, how can you split an atom without poking it?' retorted Catherine Case over her shoulder, pushing her way towards the glowing rock.

Doctor X stopped briefly in his tracks. She had made an annoyingly good point.

'Well,' he went on, 'do you think they sent the first humans to the moon by just "having a poke about"? Did Neil Armstrong step out of the lunar module and say, "That's one small step for man, one giant poke about for mankind"? Hmm? What are you doing?'

Catherine Case wasn't listening to him. She was approaching the meteorite, clambering across the deep furrows it had left in the ground. And, as he watched in horror, she reached out a finger and prodded its smooth surface firmly.

'There, you see?' she shouted up the slope. 'I'm having a poke about, and look! Nothing earth-shattering has happened.'

At that point, something earth-shattering happened: a deep crack appeared along the side of the meteorite. As it opened, blindingly bright light leaked out of it, forcing both scientists to throw up their hands and cover their eyes. With the light came a strange, deep thrumming noise that made the whole mountainside vibrate. Small landslides were released, and rocks came bouncing down the hill on either side of them.

'See?' Doctor Xavier shouted furiously. 'This is what happens when you poke about! This is what comes of not following the rules! You should ALWAYS . . . FOLLOW . . . THE RULES! FOLLOWING . . . THE RULES . . . IS . . .'

'BORING!' finished Catherine Case at the top of her voice. And, at that moment, there was a gigantic silent flash of even more intense light. It billowed up the hillside like a tidal wave, bending trees and shrubs before it as it washed over Doctor Xavier Arden and Catherine Case, knocking them both to the ground.

After a few seconds, Doctor X opened his eyes. Mentally, he scanned his body for injuries and was rather surprised to find out that he appeared to be completely unhurt.

More than that, he felt positively well. In fact, he realized, he felt so full of energy that he almost expected to see it crackling round him like electricity. He looked about him and was surprised and a little alarmed to see that he was actually covered in crackling bolts of energy.

'That's odd,' he said softly, sitting up.

A little further down the slope, Catherine Case was also sitting up, and was also, he could see, coated in the same web of bright, sparkling energy.

'Wow!' she said, leaping to her feet and doing a few star jumps. 'I don't know what's in that thing, but I want another blast of it! I feel incredible!'

She skipped down the slope to the still-glowing meteorite and, as Doctor Xavier watched in shock, picked it up as easily as if it had been an empty cardboard box.

'Check this out!' she said in delight. 'I'm a superhero!

No, not a superhero,' she went on, flexing her arms like a weightlifter and bench-pressing the meteorite. 'They're boring. They follow the rules, like you. You can be the boring hero. I'll be your evil nemesis. Here, catch, boring hero guy.'

And, with that, she threw the meteorite lightly to Doctor X. Without thinking, he caught it.

'How extraordinary!' he marvelled.

You'd think he'd be slightly more freaked out by this turn of events, but remember, he's a top scientist. He believed that top scientists should take things in their stride, rather than gasping and running about every time they made an amazing discovery. Doctor Xavier Arden would have found that very un-scientist-y.

'Extraordinary? Good name! You should use that,' suggested Catherine Case. 'You can be Doctor Extraordinary.'

'What does that make you? Captain Chaos?' asked the brand-new superhero drily.

'I quite like that, actually,' replied the newly named Captain Chaos.

*

'And that,' said the ghost of Doctor Extraordinary, back in the pedalo, 'is how it all began. That blast of energy from the mysterious meteorite gave us both super strength, and filled us with a strange energy force. But the thing about superpowers, of course, is what you choose to do with them. Will you use them for good, or will you use them for naughtiness? I, of course, became the defender of Paragon City, who always plays by the rules. And Catherine Case . . .'

'. . . thinks the rules are boring.' Sonny completed the sentence for him.

149

'Hence . . . naughty.'

'Precisely,' said the ghost. 'And that is exactly what made her so dangerous.'

He squinted out across the lake towards the city and the dark mountains beyond.

'I wonder what happened to her team of evil scientists, out there in Castle Chaos. They were always cooking up some kind of mischief.'

'Giant robots mostly,' said Sonny.

'Well, yes,' agreed the doc reluctantly. 'It mostly was giant robots. And now Paragon City has other dangers to face. How will it survive without a hero to protect it?'

'Time's up!' bellowed the gormless teenager through a megaphone. 'Time's up!'

'Well, exactly,' said Doctor Extraordinary, looking pensive. 'Couldn't have put it better myself. And that's what worries me.'

And he continued to brood anxiously as Sonny, steering constantly to the right, pedalled them one-sidedly back towards the shore.

CHAPTER 6
THE TROJAN PANDA

When cute animals feature on the news, it's usually at the end of the programme. 'And finally,' the newsreader will say, 'the heart-warming story of Bunty, the rabbit with one leg, who heroically saved her owner when he fell down a disused well.' But, when the cute animals feature right at the start of the news, you know something really very weird indeed is going on.

'Very strange breaking news on *Good Morning Paragon* today,' said Susie Carpenter, looking seriously down the camera lens. 'As the city prepares for Saturday's Hero Day parade, we're getting multiple reports that adorable baby pandas have been discovered all over the place. Let's go live to our reporter Ben Bailey now, who's on the lookout for these unusual invaders.'

'Thanks, Susie.'

As Paragon City's most fearless roving reporter, Ben Bailey had been rushed off his feet in the weeks since Doctor Extraordinary's sad accident. The crime wave that had hit the city provided him with a seemingly never-ending stream of dramatic bank robberies, hold-ups and kidnappings to cover.

When he'd got the call early this morning that the lead item on today's news would be an invasion of super-cute baby pandas, he hadn't exactly been enthusiastic about covering the story. So, as the camera cut to him at this point, he was wearing a rather angry and frustrated expression. An expression that said, *I'm a proper hard-news reporter. This panda nonsense is completely beneath me.*

Ben had got his camera operator to set up her equipment on the edge of Paragon Park, near several large flower beds and an ornamental duck pond.

'Well, as you say, this really is a very strange and – let's face it – rather ridiculous story,' he went on in the hushed tones of a wildlife presenter. 'Some might say it doesn't really qualify as news at all.' He threw a cross look at the camera. 'But overnight it does seem that the city has been flooded with small pandas. And if you look behind me –' he gestured to the camera operator and she zoomed in – 'you should be able to see one of them right now.'

Sure enough, sitting in the flower bed and eating one of the roses, was the fuzziest, big-eyedest baby panda that you ever saw. As the camera panned in, it uttered a series of tiny squeaking noises and wrinkled its little nose.

'As you can see,' said Ben Bailey wearily, 'these baby pandas really are incredibly endearing. Nobody seems to have any idea where they came from, what they're doing here or what their intentions are. Earlier I spoke to the head of the Paragon Wildlife Park . . .'

As the red light on top of the camera flicked off, Ben sighed, hoping he'd soon get called away to cover

153

a nice juicy police chase or something. Sure, the little pandas were cute, but there wasn't really anything newsworthy going on here.

They don't even have guns mounted in their mouths, he thought to himself glumly. *Or laser eyes or anything.*

A man appeared on screen, with a caption declaring that he was the HEAD OF THE PARAGON WILDLIFE PARK.

'I have no idea where they came from,' he said. 'Nor do I know what they are doing or what their intentions are.'

'So, as you can see, Susie,' Ben continued, 'some confusion this morning about where the pandas came from, what they're doing . . .'

Susie Carpenter cut him off. 'Yes, thank you, Ben,' she said a little sharply.

'But they are incredibly

154

charming,' he went on, 'and, for a city that's been hit by a crime wave since the untimely end of Doctor Extraordinary, they really do seem to be cheering people up.'

The camera panned back to show a group of people lining up to take selfies with the panda in the background. As they did so, it waddled out of the flower bed and climbed into one woman's lap, squeaking adorably to a chorus of *ahh*'s.

Sonny and his dad – along with Doctor Extraordinary – were watching all this over breakfast.

'*Ahh*, look at the pandas,' said Officer Dusty, buttering a muffin. 'Where did they come from?'

'Well, that's what nobody seems to be properly worried about,' said Sonny. 'What if it's some kind of plot?'

After years of consuming Doctor Extraordinary magazines, he knew that most unexpected

155

things did in fact generally turn out to be a plot of one sort or another.

'No need to worry about that, son,' said his dad, reaching for the teapot. 'The only person who ever plotted against Paragon City was Captain Chaos. And she's gone, thank goodness.'

'Something rather worrying has just occurred to me,' said Doctor Extraordinary, who had been gazing rather wistfully at the muffin. It was one of the things he missed most about being a ghost. Eating, that is – not muffins specifically. 'It strikes me that if I'm still here as a ghost, maybe Catherine is, too.'

'Catherine Case?' said Sonny under his breath, so his dad couldn't overhear. 'You mean . . .'

'Captain Chaos, yes,' said the doc. 'What if she's also a ghost? These pandas have evil plot written all over them.'

Sonny pondered the panda on screen, idly wondering what it would be like if it did actually have the words 'evil plot' written all over it. But the doc was right, he realized. Something did feel rather off about all this. Pandas don't just appear out of nowhere.

Imagine if they did. Weird, right?

'How would the ghost of Captain Chaos get hold of a load of pandas, though?' he asked, forgetting to whisper this time.

'What?' said his dad. 'Ghost? What on earth are you talking about?'

'Sorry,' Sonny said. 'Just thinking out loud.'

'It's an excellent question,' agreed the doc, looking out of the window and frowning at a small group of pandas that were ambling down the pavement opposite. 'And we're the only people in Paragon who suspect the city might be in danger. They all think this is some kind of . . . I don't know . . .'

'So – a clever advertising campaign?' said Susie Carpenter on the TV, as if she was answering his unspoken question. 'Some kind of effort to make Hero Day extra special? After all, it is the first one since the loss of Doctor Extraordinary. Only time will tell. But for now it's safe to say that life in Paragon City on this Wednesday morning just got a whole lot cuter. Right, Ben?'

'That's right, Susie,' replied Ben reluctantly.

The camera cut back to him in the park, where he

was now cuddling the little panda from the flower bed, which was licking his face like a puppy and blinking its huge eyes. His camera operator had persuaded him to pick it up, saying it would make a great shot, but Ben couldn't help feeling that being filmed with a baby panda licking your face was somehow demeaning for a serious journalist such as himself.

Back in Castle Chaos, PANDAmonium watched a bank of monitor screens in delight. Each one showed the live feed from the eyes of the robot pandas – one of them

was currently screening Ben Bailey's face, which was grimacing as the panda licked it.

'Excellent,' she said and cackled, rubbing her hands together in the approved villainous manner. 'This is excellent. Those idiots don't suspect a thing. I've flooded their entire city with my robots, and they just think it's some kind of treat.' She gave a louder and slightly more evil laugh.

'And what is Phase Two of the plan?' came a voice from behind her. The ghost of Captain Chaos had drifted silently through the control-room wall, her jester's hat appearing first, which would have been extremely creepy if anyone had been paying attention. 'I mean, there is another phase, right?' she went on.

'Of course there is!' snapped PANDAmonium. 'What kind of evil plan would it be without a Phase Two?'

She pointed triumphantly to a control panel beneath the monitor screens. A large red button was positioned in the very centre, with a sticky label beside it reading

Phase Two.

'Ah yes,' said Captain Chaos. 'Very good. Just checking. So, when we're ready to activate the giant panda . . .'

'You mean the *GIANT* giant panda?' said PANDA-monium.

'Yes, yes,' said Captain Chaos, waving impatiently. 'When we're ready to activate the GIANT giant panda, you will commence Phase Two by pressing that button. And?'

There was a pause. 'And what?' asked PANDAmonium eventually.

Captain Chaos sighed. 'And when you press the button,' she said, 'what *exactly* will happen?'

'I thought I'd explained that already,' said PANDAmonium. 'When I press the button, it will activate Phase Two. It's written quite clearly on the sticky label.'

'Yes,' said Captain Chaos patiently, 'but what actually is it? I mean, what will happen? Do the robot pandas do something? Have they got lasers in them? Do they all explode? Do they combine together to form a huge, destructive mega-panda?'

PANDAmonium considered these ideas. They were all superb and very evil. In hindsight, she kind of wished she'd thought of them herself when she was originally designing the robot pandas, but it was too late now.

'Let's just say,' she told the captain in a sinister tone of voice, 'that people will realize these baby pandas they like so much are not so cute after all. *A-ha. A-ha. A-ha-ha-ha-ha!* Come on – join in with the evil laughter, can't you? It's not so much fun doing it on your own. That's better. A-HA-HA-HA-HAAAAA!'

Captain Chaos, slightly reluctantly, added her own evil laughter into the mix. But she was unable to shake a slight feeling of uncertainty that her second in command had, once again, concentrated too hard on the panda aspects of the plan without sufficient emphasis on the more evil bits. *Ah well*, she thought to herself. There was always the giant giant panda robot she'd just been checking on downstairs. It was extremely large, very well-built and, despite being a panda, it really did look rather evil.

'Is that you, Sonny?' called a voice as Sonny left his flat and made for the lifts.

He ducked inside Miss Abigail's door to see the old lady curled up beside the high windows as usual, needle in hand as she worked on the enormous quilt that spilled over the sides of her armchair.

'What's going on with all these pandas, then?' she asked. 'I've just been watching the news. It sounds like one of those stories you used to tell me about Doctor Extraordinary. He'd have suspected a plot, you know.'

'This lady really is extremely wise,' said the doc approvingly, having wandered in through the wall.

'He certainly would, Miss Abigail,' agreed Sonny. 'And so do I. And I bet Spot does, too.'

'Who's Spot?' She paused in her needlework to look at him with a slight smile.

'She's, erm . . .'

He thought for a moment. Since proposing their temporary arrangement, as she insisted on calling it, he and Spot had been spending a lot of time together. She still wasn't convinced that he could see a ghost, but after hours of conversation she had at least stopped insisting he was just imagining the whole thing.

'I need more data,' is all she would say.

'She's just a girl in my class,' he told Miss Abigail finally. 'She's super smart. I bet she's got some good

ideas about where these pandas come from.'

As Sonny walked to the station, the streets of Paragon City still looked dingy and uncared for, and the train that took him round the Loop to Paragon Central was still grimy and smeared with graffiti, but suddenly nobody seemed to care. Everyone was too distracted by the adorable baby pandas that wandered here and there, peeking in through windows, clambering up drainpipes and rolling around on lawns. They seemed to be using the whole city as one giant soft-play area.

It was the same story at school. Sonny came through the front gates to find that a large crowd had gathered in the playground, all pointing to a small patch of lawn and flower beds off to one side.

'Look!' said Mr Marston, beckoning Sonny over. 'It's doing a little dance!'

Sure enough, one of the pandas was in the middle of the grassy area. It had risen up on to its stubby little hind legs and was shuffling around rhythmically, squeaking out a little song. As Sonny stepped closer he could make out some of the lyrics:

'Everybody stop,
Everybody rock,
It's time to do the Panda Pop.'

'That is the coolest thing I have ever seen,' said blue-haired Saoirse Thomas, immediately beginning to copy it.

Before long, most of the crowd – Mr Marston included – were dancing round the playground doing the

Panda Pop. Sonny glanced over at Doctor Extraordinary and rolled his eyes before looking around automatically for Spot. He saw her racing through the gates, pen in mouth as usual, and waved to catch her attention.

'Something's not right about these pandas!' they both said at the same time as she approached him.

'Such smart children,' said Doctor Extraordinary approvingly.

'The doc says we're very smart,' Sonny told Spot. 'He thinks there's something off about this panda invasion as well. It smells like a plot to me.'

'That's a highly unscientific statement,' Spot said, pulling him to one side to dodge a crowd of Panda-Popping students who were surging in their direction. In a quiet corner of the playground, she turned to face him.

'All right, then,' she said. 'Just suppose for a moment that you really can hear Doctor Extraordinary. Which, due to insufficient data, I do not accept for one second. But, just assuming you can, what does he have to say about these pandas?'

'He thinks it's Captain Chaos at work,' said Sonny, lowering his voice dramatically.

'Oh great,' said Spot. 'Now you think there are two ghosts? I could write a whole book about you, you know.'

'I do admire this young lady's respect for scientific method,' said the doc testily, 'but it is slightly wearying spending so much time with someone who doesn't believe in you.'

Sonny nodded at him sympathetically. After four weeks insisting that the doc hadn't really been in that explosion, he knew the feeling exactly.

'So what does *Doctor Extraordinary* –' Spot sketched imaginary quote marks in the air at this point – 'think the big evil plan might be?'

'I don't know,' mused the doc, wandering away from them slightly and staring once again at the dancing panda. 'I can't work out exactly what's going on, but I know someone who will.'

'Who?' said Sonny.

'What?' asked Spot.

'I said "who",' Sonny replied.

'Who? Why?' asked Spot.

(This is an example of how frustrating it can be when you're dealing with a ghost that only one person is able to hear. It can make for some very confusing and often rather tedious conversations, and we're only sorry that you had to sit through that one.)

'The doc just said, "I can't work out exactly what's going on, but I know someone who will,"' Sonny explained.

'Who?' Spot wanted to know.

'That's what I said,' said Sonny. 'Who? Who?'

'The most brilliant scientist in all of Paragon City,' declared Doctor Extraordinary in response to this brief owl impression. 'My old friend and the brains behind my whole operation, Professor Lana Holliday.'

'Lana Holliday!' exclaimed Sonny. 'Of course!'

'The brilliant scientist and the inventor of all Doctor Extraordinary's gadgets? The person who worked out how to harness his mysterious meteorite energy to power his fleet of vehicles?' said Spot, her eyes shining. She didn't have much time for superhero stories, but she was fascinated by the science parts. 'But how will we get to see her?'

'Tell your friend not to worry,' said the doc soothingly. 'If I go with you to Extraordinary Island, I'm sure we'll be able to convince her to listen to you.'

Sonny's head buzzed with excitement at the thought of visiting the actual headquarters of his hero. 'Are you sure they'll believe me, though?' he asked, slightly doubtfully.

'Of course!' the doc reassured him. 'Something about this whole panda business just doesn't feel right.'

Once again, he frowned as he looked towards the school. By now, the panda had clambered up on to a windowsill and was putting on a full dance performance, wiggling its ears and squeaking out its catchy little tune:

> '*See us here,*
> *See us there,*
> *Poppin' pandas everywhere.*'

'I have a feeling Paragon City is in danger,' Doctor Extraordinary declared dramatically. 'It's time for me to go home.'

CHAPTER 7
THE GHOST iN THE MACHiNE

'The next departure from wharf three will be the ten-oh-five Island-Hopper Service,' announced a bored-sounding voice over the tannoy. 'Calling at Fisherman's Bight, Extraordinary Island, Pine Tree Island, Dawn Lookout and Sunrise Haven.'

Sonny and Spot pushed their way through the crowd of day-trippers, many of them clutching picnic boxes and blankets. Doctor Extraordinary picked his way through behind them. As a ghost, he didn't, strictly speaking, have to weave through the throng of people as he was able to walk straight through them. But, after doing that by accident a few times, he'd explained to Sonny what an alarming experience it was.

'I got a really close look at this guy's earwax,' he had explained. 'I mean, a really, *really* close look.' His face contracted into an expression of horror at the memory. 'Never again.'

At wharf three, a smartly dressed steward checked their tickets as they thumped up the gangplank before taking their places on a wooden bench seat near the front of the blue-and-white-painted ferry.

With a puff of black fumes from the engine and a sustained parp from its whistle, the boat began to slide smoothly away from the dock. Waves slapped against the metal hull, and a sharp wind blew off the lake, whipping Spot's hair across her face and reddening Sonny's cheeks. Doctor Extraordinary had taken up a position at the front of the ferry, standing at the rail in a dramatic pose and gazing out over the sparkling waters of Lake Sunrise as the morning sun flicked up at him from countless wavelets.

'OK there, Doc?' shouted Sonny over the noise of the engines.

The doc turned and gave his trademark thumbs-up

salute, though his expression looked distracted and slightly mournful.

It must be slightly odd going back to your superhero HQ as a ghost, Sonny thought to himself.

Several picnicking families got off at the ferry's first stop, Fisherman's Bight, which was a wide sandy bay just down the lakeshore from Paragon City. After leaving the rickety wooden pier there, the boat turned away from the shoreline and began rocking gently in the larger waves as it headed directly out into the lake, aiming for the low shoreline of Extraordinary Island, which was visible not far away. Peering across the bright water, Sonny could clearly see the clean white buildings of Extraordinary Headquarters behind high walls.

When the ferry moored at the shining, modern wharf, not many people headed for the gangplank. Most of Extraordinary Island was taken up by the HQ buildings and was out of bounds to the public. Only a few wide, grassy lawns and the island's rocky western shore were accessible. Sonny saw a few men and women carrying fishing tackle heading in that direction, but apart from them he and Spot were the only people who got off – the only living people, that is.

Doctor Extraordinary walked on to the dock alongside them, looking around with a mournful expression. With a curt gesture, he beckoned the two of them towards an exit that said:

HQ THIS WAY. STRICTLY NO ADMITTANCE UNLESS ON EXTRAORDINARY BUSINESS.

'Are you absolutely sure they're going to let us in?' said Sonny nervously, jogging a little to keep up with his hero as he strode along a passageway and out on to a large, immaculately kept lawn.

'Of course they will,' the doc reassured him. 'This is my home!'

'He says they will,' Sonny told Spot.

'Why didn't your supposed ghost come here straight away, in that case?' she wanted to know. 'That would have been the scientific thing to do.' She looked up at the white walls of the HQ buildings, chewing her pen thoughtfully.

'I did,' replied the doc sadly, thinking back to his very first day as a ghost.

He'd found himself on a deserted street in the north of Paragon City, unable to remember exactly how he'd got there. With no sign of the Extra-Jet or anyone to help him, he'd made straight for the dock and boarded a ferry to Extraordinary Island. But, of course, nobody had been able to see or hear him. He'd spent a few hours in reception, shouting uselessly at the security guards, but when Lana Holliday had walked past him – and, indeed, partly through him – without so much as a second glance, the realization had hit him. He had no possible way of communicating with his team.

Sadly, he'd made his way back to the mainland to begin his search for anyone who might be able to see him. And now he had found that person he was full of confidence that the staff at his headquarters would welcome him back with open arms.

As Sonny looked out across the open space that led up to the entrance to Extraordinary HQ, though, he couldn't help thinking that the doc's confidence might be ever so slightly misplaced.

As Doctor Extraordinary's biggest fan, he knew this place inside out. He'd never actually been inside, but one issue of the fan-club magazine, *Extraordinary Weekly*, a couple of years ago had been a special edition all about it. The centre spread of the magazine was still tacked to Sonny's bedroom wall, showing in detail the laboratories, workshops, hangars, training assault courses and living quarters that made up the imposing white buildings.

Sonny also knew that the HQ employed its own security staff, trained to keep unwanted eyes away from the secret work that went on inside. And he was equally aware that no civilian who was not a member of the superhero's staff had ever been granted access – not even the leader of the whole country, who had asked for a tour on more than one occasion and been politely but firmly turned down. The technology that had been developed for Doctor Extraordinary was top, top secret.

'Come on,' said Doctor Extraordinary confidently, leading the way towards the gates, which were surrounded by a gaggle of people. 'I wonder what they're doing here,' he mused as he strode up the path, which had neatly trimmed lawns on either side.

As they drew nearer, Sonny could see that the group of

people seemed to be staging a demonstration or protest of some kind. Mainly tattily dressed, some of them were holding up banners or clutching home-made cardboard signs in front of them.

THE DOC LIVES! he read on one.
TELL THE TRUTH! urged another.

'At least some people still believe in me,' sighed Doctor Extraordinary. 'Although a lot of them used to hang around here when I was still . . . you know. Less transparent.' He grimaced as he seemed to recognize one or two faces. 'That's why I had to stop using the main gate – too many fans. One of them even used to claim we were secretly married.' He tutted. 'It seems my death hasn't put them off.'

'Do you believe?' asked a small man breathily, rushing up to them. He was wearing a T-shirt bearing a picture of the doc beneath the words **HE'LL BE BACK**.

'Believe what?' asked Spot matter-of-factly.

'Believe the truth, of course!' said the man incredulously. 'That the whole accident was staged! That the doc is still out there somewhere!'

'Looks like you've found your people,' she told Sonny

with a slight smile. 'Did you bring your placard?'

More protesters accosted them as they made their way through the knot of people towards the gates of the hero's headquarters, which were high, metal and very firmly closed.

'I know the doc's just waiting for the right moment to come back,' one woman told Sonny, running a hand through her long, tangled hair. 'I'm not supposed to tell anyone, but we were actually secretly married. I know he wouldn't just abandon me like that.'

'That's her!' said Doctor Extraordinary in surprise. 'Told you! Listen to me, madam,' he said to the woman, pushing his face close to hers. 'We are NOT married to each other! Pull yourself together!'

'She can't hear you, remember?' Sonny threw the words over his shoulder as he and Spot pushed closer to the intercom, which was fastened to one of the thick black gateposts.

Muttering crossly, the doc came to join them as Sonny stabbed a finger on a large button bearing a picture of a bell.

There was a prolonged bleep, followed by a burst

of static. 'Hello?' said a wary-sounding voice from the speaker.

'Good morning,' said Sonny politely and firmly, just as they'd planned. 'I need to speak to Professor Lana Holliday urgently, please.'

There was silence except for a low crackle that told him the person on the other end of the intercom was still listening.

'It's urgent,' said Sonny, a little more uncertainly.

'Look, how many times have I told you people?' said the voice suddenly. 'You have got to stop wasting our time like this. Please stop pressing the intercom button, or we'll send security out there to move you along.'

'I'm not wasting your time!' protested Sonny hotly. 'I told you – I've got urgent information for Professor Holliday!'

'Yeah, yeah,' said the voice sarcastically. 'Let me guess – you've discovered that Doctor Extraordinary is actually still alive, right?'

'Er, well, no. Not exactly,' said Sonny, put on to the back foot slightly by this question. 'But –' he ducked his head closer to the speaker – 'he's actually here right now.

And he needs to talk to the professor.'

'Tell him I need to talk to her with very urgent urgency!' whispered Doctor Extraordinary in his ear.

'I've already told him it's urgent!' said Sonny, flailing a hand in a *don't distract me right now!* gesture. 'Sorry,' he told the intercom. 'That's actually the doc talking to me. He said to tell you he wants to talk to the professor with, what was it? Very urgent urgency. But then –' he tailed off slightly lamely – 'you know that already.'

'Wait,' said the voice. 'You've actually got the doc there with you? And he's talking to you right now?'

'Yes! Yes!' Sonny turned to the others and raised his thumbs. Finally, it seemed, the man inside the HQ building was starting to take him seriously. 'I can hear him. Nobody else can, though. He's, kind of . . .' He lowered his voice again. 'He's – you know – a *ghost.*'

There was another moment of crackling silence from the intercom speaker. Then, abruptly, a burst of hooting laughter. It sounded like several security guards were all cracking up at the same time, having been listening in to the conversation.

'Oh, that's the best one yet!' said the original voice,

between pants of mirth. 'A ghost! Amazing! Thanks so much, you've made my day. But, seriously, stay off the intercom, all right? I can't be wasting my whole shift on this nonsense!'

'But, but . . .' Sonny felt his stomach constrict with frustration. The image of his whole class at school laughing at him swam up before his eyes. 'He's here right now!'

'Tell them what I'm wearing!' urged Doctor Extraordinary. 'You're the only one who can see me! That'll prove it!'

(He was, we'll freely admit, growing slightly desperate at this point and possibly not thinking as clearly as usual.)

'He's wearing his superhero costume!' yelled Sonny into the round metal grille, aware on some level that this was not quite the incredible revelation the doc seemed to think it was, but too frazzled to think of anything else to say. 'You know, the black one. With the silver trim!'

But, with a click, the intercom cut off.

'Don't worry,' said a girl in a tomato-red knitted hat as Sonny mooched moodily away. 'They don't ever listen to me either.'

She fell into step beside him and Spot as they headed back through the crowd and across one of the wide lawns. 'I keep telling them that Doctor Extraordinary is still talking to me, and they just treat me like I'm, I dunno, delusional or something.'

'She's clearly delusional,' said the doc. 'She obviously can't really see or hear me. Look.' He danced crazily in front of the girl, waggling his fingers in his ears and blowing raspberries with his tongue out. 'See?' he told Sonny triumphantly. 'Not a clue!'

'That's not very helpful,' Sonny told him.

'I know, right?' The girl had naturally thought Sonny was talking to her. 'I mean, he might have, like, really important information for them, you know? And every time I try and get in touch with them they just tell me to get lost. I know Marsha and Andy have had the same problems.' She gestured towards the crowd, which was now behind them.

'Marsha and Andy?' asked Spot.

'Yeah, he talks to them, too,' the girl replied. 'In fact, loads of us are still getting messages from the doc. He's definitely still out there somewhere.' She waved vaguely at the open waters of the lake. '*Definitely*. Aren't you, Doc?'

At this point, she squinted, with a sudden expression of surprise, over Sonny's shoulder towards the place where Doctor Extraordinary was, in fact, standing. But after peering for a moment she gave a small shake of her head. Then, with a nod of farewell, she moved back to join the group of protesters by the gates.

'Well, that couldn't really have gone any worse, could it?' said Sonny, flopping down on to the warm grass. 'We thought we'd get their attention if we told them I could talk to the doc. Turns out every oddball in Paragon City's already here, saying exactly the same thing! And *don't* tell me that I've been deluded all along,' he said crossly to Spot. 'You've got all the data you want now, OK? I'm clearly just as confused as this lot, right?'

Spot looked at him, chewing her pen in deep thought. Then, without speaking, she sat down gently on the grass beside him and patted him on the shoulder. Sonny, who had been expecting a cutting remark about the scientific method, smiled at her gratefully.

Doctor Extraordinary was still standing, staring over at the protesters with an expression of frustration. 'Getting messages from me,' he muttered crossly. 'I wish I *could* send messages to people. I'd tell the people in there –' he pointed at his headquarters – 'to let us in! Wait a moment.' He turned to Sonny with an excited expression. 'What if I did? What if I actually went inside? I can walk through walls, you know. It's the only superpower I seem to have left,' he added, looking rather crestfallen.

'What's the point of that, though?' said Sonny. His normally optimistic outlook had been thoroughly dimmed when the security guards had mocked him. Nobody likes being laughed at, especially over an intercom – it makes it sound all tinny and impersonal. 'I'm the only one who can see you, remember? What's the point of you haunting your old buildings if nobody knows you're there?'

There was a short pause, broken only by the hubbub of talk from the gates and the soft lapping of waves from the nearby lakeshore.

'I could do the same thing I did with Kyle Lester,' the doc said suddenly, raising a finger in the air. 'Go inside and find out something nobody else knows. Then they'd have to listen to you!'

'Actually,' said Sonny thoughtfully, 'that might just

work. We need to get their attention somehow, don't we?'

'Right! Mission accepted!' said Doctor Extraordinary, looking excited. 'Onward to the unknown!'

He strode confidently away, soon disappearing through the white wall closest to them.

Professor Lana Holliday had been Doctor Extraordinary's faithful sidekick and, indeed, best friend, for twenty years. Every day since the explosion, she had continued going into Extraordinary HQ as normal, somehow feeling that keeping busy would distract her from the grief that followed her around like a hungry dog.

She lifted her walkie-talkie as she walked down a wide flight of stairs towards the large central hangar in the middle of the main headquarters building. 'Morning, security control. Holliday here. Anything to report?'

The handset crackled. 'Nothing of note, Professor,' came the voice of the head guard. 'We've had the usual jokers at the gate, of course. One of them actually claimed that the ghost of Doctor Extraordinary is here right now, on the island. Says he needs to talk to you with "very urgent urgency" apparently.' He gave a short, barking

laugh. 'I told the kid where to get off, of course.'

Lana Holliday frowned. There were always several of these calls at the gate every day, along with the countless phone messages and emails – all of them claiming that Doctor Extraordinary was still out there somewhere. But that phrase – very urgent urgency – had been a private joke between the two of them.

'How urgent is the urgency?' she used to ask Doctor

Extraordinary whenever he'd come to her with some new idea for a gadget, a vehicle or an addition to his costume.

'It's a very urgent urgency, Holliday,' he would reply.

As far as she was aware, nobody else knew about that. She smiled at the memory, but almost immediately her frown deepened. Odd that some kid had used the exact same phrase. But – she shook her head irritably – the kid had also said there was a ghost. It was all plainly ridiculous. Suppressing a sudden shiver down her back as she reached the bottom of the stairs, she pressed the palm of her hand on to a panel beside a set of giant metal sliding doors.

The doors glided back to reveal a dazzling sight. The enormous room reached right to the back of the main HQ building, and its rear wall was made entirely of glass. The hangar was set low down so the surface of the lake actually stretched across the giant window, about two thirds of the way down. On the right, a gleaming black-and-silver submarine bobbed in a glass tank, with doors to release it into the water.

In the very centre of the hangar was the Extra-Jet, its wings folded primly upward and the polished cockpit reflecting the bright sunlight that bounced in across the lake outside. Elsewhere, other vehicles were dotted around, some apparently ready for action, some partly dismantled for maintenance – motorbikes, sports cars and even a skidoo. But all were switched off and lifeless. No lights shone from the immaculate control panels. No purr or roar came from the freshly oiled engines. No gleam of headlights.

Lana wandered sadly among the silent machines, reaching out now and then to brush a hand against them as if they were old friends or rub away a smear with the sleeve of her jacket.

None of these vehicles had worked since the day Captain Chaos's robot had exploded with both her and Doctor Extraordinary inside it. The Extra-Jet had been towed back to this hangar on a lorry and a cargo boat before being winched in by crane through the circular opening in the hangar roof. Because, like all the vehicles Lana Holliday had designed for the doc to use, it worked by harnessing the mysterious energy that had been released by the strange meteorite that had given him his powers. No fuel was necessary; Doctor Extraordinary simply had to grasp the joystick, and the jet's engines would fire into life.

Lana Holliday had spent her entire career researching the strange accident that had transformed the quietly spoken scientist into a superhero. She had quickly discovered that his body was filled with an unbelievable store of energy that seemed to have no easily explained source. It gave him incredible strength and speed, but she had also managed to divert this energy to power the gadgets and vehicles she'd spent years helping him to design.

Lana had named the substance from the meteorite Q crystals, because they seemed to emit a kind of radiation known as quantum rays. But, despite all her research, she was still not able to explain exactly where the Q energy came from. And now, with Doctor Extraordinary gone, she was unable to replicate the energy and power his fleet of vehicles. It seemed that, without the doc, the entire Extraordinary operation could not continue. And Paragon City was, it seemed, slowly and unstoppably sliding into a decline without its resident saviour to give the people the hope they needed.

Lana stood stock-still as the door slid quietly closed

behind her. Hands on hips, she surveyed the silent fleet of gleaming technology scattered round the hangar and sighed.

'Oh, Doc,' she said softly to herself, 'I just can't get any of it to work without you. I'm going to have to give it up. All of it.'

Once again, she felt that strange chill down her spine. Despite the hangar being temperature-controlled and airtight, a couple of sheets of thin paper on a nearby workbench fluttered slightly. The professor turned her head sharply at the noise. Apart from her, the huge space was deserted.

'Hello?' she said uncertainly, glancing behind her.

The doors were securely shut. But another sound made her turn back into the hangar, an expression of complete disbelief spreading across her face. The noise that had attracted her attention was tiny and high-pitched; an electrical whine that would normally be lost in the other larger noises filling the giant room. But Lana knew what it was straight away. It was the small, subtle sound that the circuits of the Extra-Jet made when they were switched on.

188

Professor Lana Holliday climbed up on to a chair so she could see into the jet's cockpit. Sure enough, multicoloured lights had begun to flash on the control panel. And, as she watched, the expression on her face changing from pure disbelief into frank, delighted excitement, the jet's wings delicately folded themselves downwards like a newly hatched butterfly. As they clicked into place, Lana scrambled for the walkie-talkie on her belt.

'Security,' she said breathlessly, 'security, quickly! That kid who said the doc was here – go outside and bring him to the main hangar right now! It's urgent! In fact –' she looked once again at the apparently empty cockpit, now filled with blinking flashes of coloured light, and gave a disbelieving, quizzical but nonetheless enormous grin – 'it's very urgently urgent!'

'So he's seriously here?' asked Professor Lana Holliday. 'You can see him sitting on that chair right now?'

'Yup,' said Sonny. 'He's sticking his thumbs up. And he says he's missed you.'

'This all feels highly unscientific,' complained the professor.

'That's what I keep saying!' Spot agreed shrilly.

She had been startled when a pair of security guards had singled them out in the crowd outside Extraordinary HQ and ushered them inside. That startlement had turned to downright flabbergastery when they'd been greeted by none other than this legendary scientist and inventor. And flabbergastery had deepened into massive, head-filling bamboozlement when – instead of assuming that all talk of ghosts was unscientific and ridiculous – Lana Holliday had actually appeared to believe Sonny's claim that he could somehow see Doctor Extraordinary.

'It's all highly unscientific!' Spot said once more, sinking down on to a chair and unsnapping her notebook. But, as she poised her pen over the page, Spot realized she had absolutely no idea what to write down.

'W-R-O-N-G, if you're wondering how to spell it,' Sonny told her cheekily. 'That's what you're about to put, isn't it? "I admit I was wrong"?'

'A scientist never admits they're wrong,' replied Spot automatically.

'I used to think that, too,' Lana Holliday told her

kindly. 'But after the doc's encounter with the meteorite I had to change my opinion a bit. And I found that, once you do admit you're wrong, you often discover something rather incredible.'

Spot stared at her, open-mouthed, looking as if her whole world had been turned upside down.

'You'll get used to it,' Lana went on, patting her on the arm.

'A ghost, though?' said Spot. 'I mean . . . a ghost? I've read so many books about all kinds of science, and not one of them mentioned ghosts.'

'Great!' said Lana with a smile. 'That means there's still a book left to be written. Good to see you're taking notes.'

Spot was still holding her pen rather shakily above the page. With an uncertain expression, she wrote the word *GHOST* at the top and underlined it.

'Excellent,' said Lana. 'Right – let's examine the data, shall we?'

Spot looked slightly relieved at hearing this word, and she jotted it down as a subheading.

'We know the Extra-Jet activated,' the professor

continued, 'and we know that, logically, that's only possible if the doc is somehow here. So – ready to science the actual heck out of this?'

'Always!' said Spot, now noticeably cheering up at the mention of another one of her favourite words. (*Science*, that is. Not *heck*.)

Sonny, meanwhile, was gazing round the hangar with the strange feeling that he'd been there before. He hadn't, of course, but he had read about this room for hours on end in *Extraordinary Weekly*. A large diagram showing all the different vehicles was pinned to his wall. There was the Extra-Speedboat, he thought to himself, looking over towards the high glass wall with the waves of the lake lapping halfway up it. And that, over there in the corner underneath a large tarpaulin, must be the gleaming black Extra-Bike.

What would his fellow Sidekicks make of this? he wondered. He was the first-ever member of the fan club to actually be allowed inside Extraordinary HQ. But there was no time for any more sightseeing. Paragon City was in danger, he reminded himself. This was a rescue mission.

Lana Holliday had placed a metal chair in the middle of a large clear space to one side of the huge room, and was now busily dragging pieces of equipment over to surround it.

'This is certainly something I didn't study at college,' she said wonderingly, positioning a metal device that looked a little like a thick telescope on a stand near the chair.

'Sorry,' said Sonny.

'Don't be!' Lana told him. 'I mean, what fun would life be if you learned everything you needed to know in school, right? I hope I never stop running across new mysteries. Though as mysteries go –' she flicked a switch on the side of the machine – 'this is, without question, something of a biggie.'

'What's that she's got there?' asked Doctor Extraordinary, who was sitting on the chair with an excited expression. 'A ghost detector?'

He was thrilled to be back at Lana Holliday's side again, and in fact had turned away a couple of times to prevent Sonny seeing a few ghostly tears leaking out. The thought that Lana's technology might actually enable her to see him once again was cranking up his excitement to fever pitch.

'I don't think there's any such thing as a ghost detector,' Sonny told him, and Lana grinned again.

'This is something I invented when I was trying to find out what substance those crystals are made of,' she said. 'I just call it the Q-Scope. Now let's have a look.'

She moved behind the device and pressed a button. A screen on the back end of the tube lit up, and she gasped.

'Come and look at this!' she told them.

Sonny and Spot rushed round to the back of the tube, but the screen was simply showing a normal-looking image of the chair.

'That's funny,' said Lana, tapping the screen with a finger. 'A moment ago, there was a load of Q energy clustered round the chair.'

Sonny felt a slight chill on the back of his neck and realized what had happened. 'When she said come and look at this,' he told the doc, who had also come to investigate and was now standing behind him, peering over his shoulder, 'I don't think she meant you. It's you we're supposed to be looking at, remember?'

'Ah yes,' said Doctor Extraordinary, holding up a hand in apology. 'I'll go back and sit down, shall I? Yes, mission accepted. Onward to the unknown!'

He strode back to the chair, and now it was Sonny and Spot's turn to gasp in astonishment. A faint dancing collection of purple dots, like minuscule butterflies, was flickering around the metal chair on the screen.

'This device measures Q energy,' Lana told them. 'And, as you can see, there's a lot of it around that chair – which is where the doc is now standing, right?'

'He's doing a little dance of some kind, actually,' said Sonny.

Doctor Extraordinary, apparently totally delighted that someone else now believed in his existence, was moonwalking backwards round the chair, doing jazz hands.

Spot had been about to write something down in her notebook, but instead she stopped. Putting her pen back in her mouth, she looked in amazement at the pattern of dancing purple dots on the screen.

'I was wrong,' she said faintly.

'Boom!' said Sonny, which was slightly unkind – but

give him a break. It's tough spending weeks claiming you can see a ghost with nobody believing you.

'Well done,' Lana told Spot. 'You've just taken your first step into a larger universe.'

'There actually is a ghost,' Spot went on. 'You were right, Sonny. Doctor Extraordinary really is still here.'

And, as she spoke, a shape coalesced in the air beside the metal chair. It started out indistinct, almost like a trick of the light. Spot felt as if her focus was adjusting, like the feeling when you go cross-eyed. And then suddenly she could see him. Her mouth hung open, her pen spiralling down to clatter on the hangar floor.

'Hello, Spot,' said Doctor Extraordinary.

'I can hear him, too! He's here!' Spot gasped. 'He's real!'

And, as if those words had given her brain permission to accept it, Lana Holliday reached up and rubbed her own bedazzled eyes as the doc appeared for her, too, smiling and raising a thumb in his trademark salute.

'I don't believe it!' she said without thinking.

'Well, they say seeing is believing,' replied Doctor Extraordinary. 'Although let's not forget there's someone here who believed without seeing. That's even more special.'

Sonny felt himself blush as the other three turned to look at him with smiles of warm affection.

For the first time since he'd been blown up, Doctor Extraordinary was starting to feel like a hero again. He exchanged a smile with Sonny, the boy who'd refused to accept he was gone, before turning to Spot, who despite her doubts had kept on wondering, always wanting to know more. And finally he rested his gaze on his old friend and advisor, Professor Lana Holliday, whose eyes were filled with rather unscientific tears.

'Good to be back,' said the doc with a slight catch in his voice.

'Good to have you back.'

Lana's expression held more words than any emotional speech could have done. (Which was lucky because this scene is in danger of getting overly mushy. Let's get on with the adventure, shall we?)

'OK.' Lana Holliday turned to Sonny and Spot, looking suddenly businesslike. 'So why did the doc bring you to see me? What's so very urgently urgent?'

'Oh yes!'

In all the excitement, Sonny had completely forgotten the reason they'd come to talk to the professor in the first place.

'It's the pandas!' he told her. 'We think that if Doctor Extraordinary is, you know, still here . . .'

'Hello,' broke in the doc, waving. He was still full of excitement that two more people could now see and hear him. Spot and Lana waved back.

'We think that if the doc's still here,' Sonny continued, 'then Captain Chaos might be, too. And we think it's her that's sending the pandas!'

'Hmm.' Lana Holliday grabbed a newspaper from a nearby desk.

On the front was a picture of several of the baby pandas clustered on a street corner, beneath the headline:

INVASION OF THE ADORABLES!
City goes into cuteness overload as mystery fluff bundles delight Paragon

said a smaller line of print underneath.

'They don't look particularly evil,' said Lana doubtfully.

'Well, exactly, Holliday!' said the doc. 'That's what makes it such a dastardly plan! I mean, you wouldn't invade the city with some evil-looking animal, would you? It would be too obvious!'

'Yeah, like aardvarks or something,' said Spot. Everyone turned to stare at her.

'What's so evil about aardvarks?' asked Sonny after a pause.

Spot sniffed. 'I just don't trust them,' she said. 'Something weird about the way their noses wiggle about.'

'Right, here's the plan,' said Lana, keen to get things moving before the conversation got sidetracked with too much aardvark-based discussion. 'The doc stays here with me, and I'll try and figure out what on earth – or indeed off earth – is going on.'

'Roger,' said Sonny, an excited feeling filling him up like a fizzy drink at the prospect of doing real superhero stuff inside an actual superhero headquarters. 'And what about me and Spot? What's our mission?'

'Ah well, you two have a very important assignment,' Lana told him, increasing the excited feeling by a factor of at least 7.8. 'You two, capture one of those baby pandas and bring it here. Let's see what's really going on, shall we?'

'Mission accepted!' Sonny saluted smartly, before uttering a sentence that should never be used in any circumstances other than these exact ones:

'Come on, Spot – let's go panda-hunting!'

CHAPTER 8
HUNTING PANDAS IN PARAGON PARK

S onny burst into his flat an hour and a half later, with Spot in tow.

'Right,' she said. 'No time to lose.'

Spot was incredibly excited that a real-life top scientist had given her an important mission. 'Let's grab what we need, get out there and catch that panda!'

Sonny looked around him. 'What exactly do you take on a panda-hunting expedition?' he wondered out loud.

'Item one: a large net,' said Spot firmly. 'Where does your dad keep his nets?'

(This sounds like a strange question, but it might help to point out that both Spot's parents were scientists.

In fact, her dad was a zoologist who studied butterflies and beetles. He had a whole collection of different-sized nets. Actually, now we come to think about it, they really should have gone to Spot's house at this point in the story. But they didn't.)

Sonny looked at her for a moment. 'I don't think we've got, like, a special cupboard full of nets or anything,' he told her. Spot snorted with disapproval at this oddness. 'But I'm sure I brought one back from holiday once. It'll be with the other beach stuff. Come on.'

He led the way down the corridor and threw open the double doors of the large storage cupboard opposite his dad's bedroom.

Inside was a bewildering variety of things. Towards the front, because they were needed the most often, was the Hoover, the mop and bucket and the other cleaning stuff. But behind them, clustered together and largely forgotten, were all the things that Sonny and his dad owned, but only needed approximately once a year or less.

You probably have a similar space in your own house. Go and have a peek at it now, but take the book with you so you can keep reading. Looks like a total mess, doesn't it? The Christmas decorations are in there somewhere, probably in about three boxes plus an overflow bag for the stray bits of tinsel that nobody spotted until February.

There's also bound to be a bag of old Halloween costumes; some toys your parents couldn't bring themselves to throw away; and somewhere, right at the back, a tin of paint that was there when you moved in and will probably still be there a hundred years from now when this book is rightfully hailed as a classic.

Anyway, we're getting sidetracked looking in the cupboard. But also in there somewhere there's sure to be a container of beach stuff. It may have buckets and spades; it may have a beach umbrella. It definitely has a load of sand in the bottom that will tip out all over your feet when you try and get anything out of it. And, in Sonny's case, it also contained a long bamboo pole with a wide green net at one end.

His dad had bought it when they'd gone crabbing at the seaside a couple of years back – they'd caught a crab, which Sonny had named Plimpy and kept in a bucket for half an hour until his dad made him release it back into the sea. But the tale of Plimpy the crab will have to wait (possibly for a picture book – let's ask the Chief Puffin) because it's the net we're really interested in here.

'There it is!' Sonny cried, knocking over the Hoover as he grabbed the bag of beach stuff. Sand poured over his feet as he tilted it (see previous paragraph), but he found the net and turned to Spot, holding it up in triumph.

'Excellent work,' she said. 'Now we just need some

way of getting the panda to Extraordinary Island without attracting too much attention.'

'How about in that?' Sonny said, noticing an old pushchair folded up in the corner. 'We could tie it into that, cover it up with a blanket and say it's, you know, our baby brother or something.'

'Brilliant!' exclaimed Spot. 'You've got quite a talent for this, you know.'

'What, secret panda kidnapping?' asked Sonny. 'Erm, well, thanks. I think.'

At that moment, the bedroom door behind them burst open, and Sonny's dad was revealed, wearing pyjama trousers, a Paragon Pirates baseball shirt and a cross expression.

'What on earth's all this noise?' he asked plaintively. 'You know I'm on nights this week!'

Sonny grimaced. 'Sorry, Dad,' he said. 'But actually it's great you're awake. Spot and I could really use your help. This is Spot, by the way.'

'Hello!' Spot waved slightly awkwardly. 'Nice jammies.'

'Spot?' Sonny's dad scratched his head and yawned.

'It's Victoria, actually,' said Spot, with the air of

someone who had to give this explanation quite a lot. 'Blott. But nobody calls me Victoria except my mum when I've been naughty. So Spot's fine. Nice to meet you.'

Sonny's dad still looked half asleep. 'What was it you just said?' he asked his son. 'You wanted my help with something?'

'Paragon City's in danger!' Sonny told him dramatically.

He'd always wanted to dramatically say that sentence so it was quite an exciting moment. But he'd been hoping for a more enthusiastic reply.

'Oh, is it?' said his dad in a disinterested tone of voice. 'Again? Nightmare. Well, I'm sure someone will deal with it. As long as they keep the noise down, I'm happy.' He turned to go back into his bedroom.

'No, Dad!' said Sonny urgently. 'This is serious. It really, really is! Doctor Extraordinary needs our help!'

'Oh, for goodness' sake, Sonny!'

His tired dad's temper had snapped like a cheap breadstick. He'd stayed up after his shift to go shopping for Miss Abigail, and had then sat chatting to her over a cup of tea when he really should have been sleeping. At this point, he'd only actually been in bed for half an hour, so we can probably forgive him for being ever so slightly tetchy.

'You've got to let this go! If there's a problem in the city, the police department will be on the case. Just like I was, *all night*.' He stressed these last two words in a way that meant *please just let me go back to bed now.*

'But the doc . . .' Sonny felt frustration boiling up inside him.

'I'm sorry, Sonny, but the doc's gone,' said his dad with finality. 'Whatever superhero story you think is going on – attack of the killer bananas, runaway bus full of bees – my colleagues will be doing their best to deal with it.'

He shook his head, grasped the door handle and prepared to shut himself away, then turned back. Perhaps there was something in this after all.

'What is this problem anyway?' he asked.

'The pandas!' declared Sonny. 'The tiny pandas! We think they're evil!'

'Oh boy,' said his dad with a sigh. 'Well, it was nice to meet you, Spot,' he added, slamming the bedroom door behind him.

Sonny stood for a moment, looking crestfallen. 'He

never wants to get involved in any of the superhero stuff,' he told Spot sadly. 'He thinks it's all a waste of time.'

Spot shuffled her feet, not quite sure what to say. 'Well,' she said, 'I know it's not a waste of time. And there's a professor who wants to be in possession of a panda, pronto! So let's go and catch one!'

'You might want to work on your superhero catchphrases,' Sonny told her as, clutching net and pushchair, they stampeded out of the flat, slamming the door rather deliberately loudly behind them.

Some time later, the two panda-hunters made their way into Paragon Park. The open spaces there, they decided, gave them the best chance of finding one of the animals and grabbing it.

'Stay alert,' muttered Sonny as they passed through a pair of high green metal gates. 'There must be one around here somewhere.'

'Over there!' said Spot suddenly, pointing. Sure enough, one of the baby pandas was waddling into the small funfair just inside the park entrance. 'After it, quick!'

Pushing the pushchair, which they had finally managed

to unfold after ten very frustrating minutes, the pair dashed after it. But, when they got to the fair, the panda was nowhere to be seen.

'It can't have gone far,' said Sonny. 'Act casual.'

It's quite hard to act casual when you're shoving a pushchair with nothing in it except a large green net, but they did their best, wandering past stalls where you could win giant cuddly toys. Further in were the bigger rides – a ghost train, a merry-go-round and some bumper cars.

'If you were a panda, where would you hide in a funfair?' said Spot thoughtfully, looking around.

'That is, without doubt, the strangest question I've ever been asked,' Sonny replied.

'Well, I'd very much like you to answer it anyway,' she said with a grin. 'The safety of Paragon City may depend on it, remember?'

'Hmmm . . .' Sonny examined the rides. 'I guess, if I was a panda, I'd probably have a ride on the bumper cars,' he said after a pause.

'Really?' Spot tilted her head in surprise. 'What makes you say that?'

'Well, it's just that I can see a panda riding in one

of the bumper cars,' answered Sonny.

They rushed over to the large oval stand where the cars were whooshing round in a clockwise direction. Sure enough, clinging to the back of one of them like a fluffy mascot was a panda. The girl driving the car seemed delighted, and was trying to take a selfie with the panda in the background. As a result, she kept crashing into other people.

'Quick, after it!' urged Spot, digging in her pocket for money.

The robot pandas that had been made at Castle Chaos had an important safety feature. They were designed to be cute, so nobody would suspect them, but they were also designed to evade capture. PANDAmonium didn't want anyone looking too carefully at her creations after all. So if one of the pandas detected pursuit, or thought someone was trying to trap it, it would immediately go into escape mode. And that's exactly what this panda did when its robot brain noticed two children driving towards it in a bumper car, one of whom was clutching a large green net.

'It's making a run for it!' shouted Spot as the panda

leaped off its own car on to another one further away from them. Bounding from car to car, it made for the side of the track as fast as its stumpy legs would carry it.

Abandoning their vehicle, despite the owner's angry shout of 'Oy! No arms and legs outside the cars, please!', Sonny and Spot gave chase.

Moving with surprising speed now that it realized it was being pursued, the panda whizzed out of the funfair and away across the park. Sonny and Spot sprinted after it as fast as they could go.

'Quick!' snapped Spot.

'I'm going quick!' Sonny panted. 'This is literally my quickest!'

Pandas don't move especially fast – not even robot ones – and, despite its frantic attempts to escape, they were gaining on this one. It was clearly making for a large patch of woodland where it would be able to lose them, and Sonny put on a frantic burst of speed to catch it before it could reach the safety of the trees.

When there were only a few metres to go, he made a desperate lunge with the net, sweeping it forward as he launched himself into the air. The net closed over the panda, but it didn't stop running. And Sonny, off balance, fell to the ground. Now he was being towed across the grass on his stomach by the still-stampeding panda, which was firmly trapped beneath the net.

'Quick! Help!' he shouted to Spot, who had fallen behind.

Just as the runaway panda reached the edge of the trees, she grabbed Sonny by the ankles and heaved. Squeaking furiously, the netted panda was dragged backwards away from its escape route, and before it could make another bid for freedom Sonny let go of the net handle and dived quickly on top of it, uttering yet another two sentences that will never become a real superhero catchphrase.

'I've apprehended the panda! Quick, get the pushchair!'

'Come on, then, little sister,' said Spot loudly and unconvincingly as she pushed the panda up the gangplank and on to the ferry. 'Time for a nice day out on the islands. Just me, my friend and my baby sister here in her buggy.'

'Don't you think you're overdoing it ever so very slightly?' asked Sonny, looking nervously from side to side.

The panda was strapped firmly into the pushchair,

with a blanket pulled right up round its head, but it wasn't going to fool anyone who decided to take a closer look. Their only hope was to stay completely inconspicuous, and Sonny didn't feel that Spot was completely filling that brief.

'My baby sister just loves a ferry ride,' said Spot airily to the ticket inspector as she deftly manoeuvred the pushchair on to the metal deck and began to wheel it towards the large open area at the back of the ferry. 'Yup, this completely normal little tyke just loves a day out on the water. Yes siree.'

'*Danger. Danger. Capture detected. Initiate defence protocol,*' came a high-pitched voice from the depths of the blanket.

'Oh, ha ha ha!' Spot laughed, a little too loudly, leaning down and smothering the panda's mouth with the flat of her hand as several other passengers looked round curiously. 'She's always playing this game. Yes, erm, Gertie, capture detected. Ha ha. Very funny. You sound just like a robot. She's very advanced,' Spot explained to a well-dressed older lady as they rushed past her towards an empty space on the deck.

'Gertie?' asked Sonny between clenched teeth. 'You've decided to call your imaginary sister Gertie?'

'I panicked,' replied Spot in a stage whisper. 'And, if you must know, Gertie was the name of my imaginary friend when I was younger. She used to go everywhere with me. Bit of company, you know.' She looked a little embarrassed.

'*Alert. Seek assistance,*' chirruped the panda in the pushchair.

'Shut up!' Spot hissed at it aggressively, before noticing that the smartly dressed lady had followed them. When she heard Spot, the friendly smile she had been wearing drained from her face like paint in the rain.

'It's just a game she plays with her sister,' said Sonny loudly. 'It's not how it sounds!'

The woman, looking slightly doubtful, moved a couple more steps towards them.

'I just wanted to say hello,' she said. 'I do love children, you see.' She made as if to bend over the pushchair, reaching a finger towards the fold of blanket that covered the panda's furry face.

'Gah, DON'T!' Spot squealed frantically.

The woman froze, the quizzical expression on her face now hardening into one of hostile mistrust.

'She's got chickenpox!' Spot blurted in a high-pitched warble like a startled goose. 'And, erm . . .'

'What my friend means,' said Sonny, shushing Spot with a glare, 'is that her little sister just got over chickenpox. So it's best not to disturb her, if that's OK?'

'*Contact Castle Chaos urgently*,' squeaked a voice from the pushchair as the woman reluctantly withdrew her finger and backed away, still looking at Sonny and Spot with narrowed eyes.

For the rest of the journey, they were forced to stand

217

right at the back of the ferry, where the roar of the engines drowned out the panda's increasingly frequent squeaks of alarm. Finally, though, they were able to disembark at Extraordinary Island and head back to the main headquarters building.

'Did you get one?' crackled the voice of Professor Lana Holliday from the intercom.

'*Danger. Capture detected,*' said the panda.

'Ah,' Lana continued, 'I think that answers my question. Right, come straight to my private laboratory. I've discovered something truly amazing about your ghost.'

CHAPTER 9
THE SHADOW ON THE WALL

Professor Lana Holliday's laboratory was a large, brightly lit room lined with cluttered desks full of the most fascinating things imaginable. There were huge sheets of blue paper with designs for vehicles and gadgets sketched on them. There were computer monitors showing rotating 3-D animations of circular blobs that might have been planets, atoms or possibly even oranges.

As they pushed their way through the rubber swing doors, Spot's eyes widened so much that it appeared as though her eyeballs wanted to pop out and start looking around without waiting for the rest of her body to get itself moving. Grabbing her notebook and pen, which she'd largely forgotten about during the panda-hunting interlude, Spot rushed over to the nearest desk with a gasp.

'What's this?' she asked, peering down a high-tech microscope. 'No, wait!' She dashed to one of the computer monitors. 'What's that? Tell me that first, then tell me about the other thing.'

'Looks like an orange,' said Sonny, peering round the room curiously.

Among all the scientific instruments and complicated designs, there was one thing that definitely didn't belong in this lab. And that was the large orange tent that had been pitched incongruously in the very centre of the floor. Doctor Extraordinary was standing beyond it, looking rather excited.

'Planning a little sleepover, are you?' Sonny asked the professor, who had marched over and was unzipping the triangular door on the end of the tent.

'I think I've worked out what's happened,' Lana Holliday explained, her eyes shining with excitement.

Spot's own eyes widened at this, and she flicked

back to the page in her book where she'd written the word GHOST as a title earlier.

'Seriously?' she said breathlessly, rushing up to Lana. 'You've worked out a scientific explanation for ghosts?'

'Well,' said the professor hesitantly, 'I think I've worked out why we can still see the doc, at least. And it's all to do with the energy that gave him his superpowers in the first place.'

'And camping?' asked Sonny, coming over to join them and examining the tent.

'I think this will help explain it to you, Sonny,' said Lana. 'Not you, Spot. You'll get it straight away. But we're not all scientific geniuses, right?'

Spot almost visibly glowed with pride as the professor ushered them both inside the tent.

Sonny and Spot clambered through the flaps to see that the professor had lined the floor with a comfortable checked rug and a few cushions. She joined them as they settled themselves on the ground, enjoying the warm orange glow cast by the bright lights of the lab shining on the canvas walls.

'This laboratory,' began Professor Holliday, sitting just

inside the tent doorway, 'represents the universe. And this tent represents the parts of the universe that you can normally see, smell, hear, touch and taste. The parts of the universe that are detectable by the human senses in other words.'

'Like cheese?' Sonny wanted to know.

'Yes, Sonny, cheese would definitely be inside the tent,' she said, nodding. 'You can taste, smell, touch and see cheese.'

'You can also hear cheese,' he added, 'if it's that squeaky stuff that you put in burgers.'

'Or if you drop it,' said Spot, who was still in a buoyant

mood after being described as a scientific genius by another scientific genius.

'I think you're getting the idea,' said the professor, smiling. 'So, inside the tent, that's the parts of the universe we can sense. But what's outside the tent?'

'Cows?' asked Sonny. 'Mum and Dad took me camping once, and when we woke up the tent was surrounded by cows.'

'Not cows, no,' Lana Holliday said. 'This is the whole universe, remember, not just a farm. So, if this room is the universe, and inside the tent is what we can see –'

'The professor is talking about the parts of the universe that we cannot usually detect,' Spot broke in kindly. 'Things like dark matter and quantum particles.'

'Exactly!' The professor beamed at Spot, who grinned back excitedly. 'Outside this tent – outside the things we can sense – is a whole range of things. Some of them can sometimes be seen by scientists. Some of them we only know to be there because of the effect they have. Some of them we just don't know about. Take quarks, for example. Do either of you know what a quark is?'

'It sounds like the noise a very posh duck makes,' said a

voice in Sonny's ear. Doctor Extraordinary had stuck his head through the tent. He snorted with laughter.

'I see your jokes haven't been improved by getting blown up,' said Lana, looking slightly pained. 'Quarks are a kind of quantum particle,' she went on.

'Quantum particles aren't visible,' Spot told Sonny, 'and they're very difficult to detect. But we scientists know they're there.'

'Right again, as usual,' Lana said, congratulating her.

'So what's this got to do with me?' asked Doctor Extraordinary.

As a former scientist, he was fascinated by the idea, but having spent the last twenty years as a superhero he was also keen to start running about, making quips.

'I was just getting to that,' said Lana. 'It's always been clear that those mysterious crystals from the meteorite affected you on a quantum level, Doc. That's why I called them Q crystals at the start of my research. Somehow, when they were exposed to that energy, both Doctor Extraordinary and Captain Chaos were linked to the quantum field, which is –' she waved a hand towards the tent doorway – 'out there. Out in the parts of the universe that we can't see. That's what gave him his powers. He existed partly inside the tent – and partly outside.'

Which, incidentally, was exactly where the doc still was, sticking oddly through the orange canvas to listen to this explanation.

'When the explosion happened,' the professor went on, 'it destroyed the parts of the doc that were inside the tent, so we can no longer see or hear him. But if you step outside into the lab, Sonny, you can help me demonstrate this.'

Sonny climbed through the doorway and heard Spot gasp. His dark shadow was beamed on to the tent wall.

'You see?' the professor was saying. 'The doc still exists in quantum space. Sonny – and now the rest of us – are seeing a kind of shadow of his quantum self projected on to our reality, just like that shadow on the tent wall.'

Spot had been writing so fast that Sonny was slightly surprised not to see smoke coming off the end of her pen. 'This is incredible,' she said softly. 'Doctor Extraordinary was made into a multidimensional being by the Q energy. So even though he got blown up in this dimension . . . he's still out there.'

'Cutting-edge science, for sure,' said Lana in agreement.

'And we can see him as an echo from quantum space,' Spot went on.

'Why was it only me that could see him, though?' asked Sonny suddenly from outside the tent.

'I don't know,' said Lana Holliday musingly.

'Well, that's not a very encouraging thing for a scientist to say,' Spot told her.

'Actually,' said the professor, 'they're the most exciting three words a scientist can ever say. When scientists stop saying, "I don't know," then science will be over! I'd far rather discover a brand-new mystery than solve an old one.'

Spot thought about this for a moment. 'Actually,' she said, 'that's absolutely right, isn't it?'

Lana Holliday smiled. 'But I can suggest an answer,' she added. 'Think about the moment that you and I could see him, Spot.'

'It's when we believed he was there,' Spot said, reading back over her notes.

'Right,' Lana told her. 'And, at that point, our brains were able to accept what was there – almost like tuning into a certain frequency. Of course, Sonny was tuned into it all along. He was the doc's number-one fan, right? So who better to pick up those strange vibrations from quantum space that tell us that Doctor Extraordinary is still out there? Somewhere, somehow.'

Sonny felt a warm glow of pride. He, and he alone, had kept the faith after his hero had gone. And his reward was that he had been the only person in the whole world capable of seeing him – a strange, lonely shadow on the tent wall of the universe.

'Well, I think I got that,' said Doctor Extraordinary, interrupting his reverie. 'I'm an astrogeologist, not a quantum physicist, but I think it's clear. Still don't understand what any of this has got to do with ducks, though,' he added in an undertone to Sonny, who grinned.

'But what about the pandas?' said Spot after a short silence.

'Ah!' Lana Holliday led the way out of the tent and towards the panda in the pushchair. 'Good point, Spot. Let's try and find out, shall we?'

Grabbing the handles, she pushed the panda over to the side of the lab, where a series of machines and gadgets was arranged along a cluttered workbench. Once again, Spot peered at them all in fascination.

'Don't touch that one!' warned Lana as Spot wandered to the end of the bench and peered at a long, fat rocket-shaped object made of gleaming metal. Bright lights flashed from a complicated control panel on the side.

'Why?' said Spot, looking at the missile, or whatever it was, in fascination. 'What is it?'

'It's a new weapon I was working on for the Extra-Jet,' Lana explained. 'But it's just a prototype at the moment. I test-fired it the other day, and it blasted a hole in the wall.' She pointed to a large area of new brickwork on one side of the lab. 'It works by sending out powerful sound waves, but it seems to be capable of reducing brick and stone to dust. I need to work on toning it down a bit before it's ready to use.'

'Hmm,' said Spot.

(And 'hmm' says everyone reading this book as well, thinking to themselves, *I wonder if that powerful weapon might just come in useful later on in the story?* Well, more about that at the end of the chapter. Firstly, let's follow Lana and the others as they examine the panda.)

'Come on, fella,' said Lana, gently unclipping the panda from its pushchair and nudging it gently into a large metal cage. 'Let's see if we can't figure out what you are, my little friend,' she went on, moving over to a control panel beneath a large screen, 'and where you come from.'

She clicked her fingers rapidly across a keyboard, and there was a high-pitched whine as machinery started up. The panda chittered in alarm, rushing to and fro in the cage, apparently looking for a way out.

TRIGGER WARNING. The baby panda **EXPLODES** in a few paragraphs' time. If you're a panda, or a fan of pandas, and feel you might be disturbed by reading about an adorable little panda exploding, then please fetch a biscuit right now and hold it at the ready. It'll help when the time comes.

'**Danger, danger,**' chirruped the panda. '**Initiate emergency protocol.**'

Lana Holliday pressed a few more keys, and a large screen lit up, displaying a live X-ray of the sweet little animal.

'Now look here,' said Lana, pointing at the image on the screen. 'As we know, this panda is a very sophisticated robot. But it's not the first robot of its kind I've seen.'

'Captain Chaos?' asked Doctor Extraordinary and Sonny at the same time. Lana smiled.

'Exactly.' She clicked her fingers. 'It's a similar design to the Chaos robots that have been used to attack the city. The main difference, of course, is that it's much smaller.'

'And it's a panda,' added Spot.

'Well, yes,' said Lana. 'The panda thing is certainly new. Lucky it's so small really. I mean, imagine an enormous robot panda attacking Paragon City.'

There was a small nervous laugh from Sonny and Spot, but it quickly died out like a low-quality firework.

Everyone was immediately imagining the very real possibility that this might actually happen – completely correctly as it turns out.

'Anyway,' continued Lana Holliday after a moment, still typing rapidly, 'I'm now attempting to access some of this robot's programming.'

'Infiltration of panda protocols detected.' said the panda in the cage shrilly. **'Initiating self-destruct in ten seconds.'**

'Always with the self-destruct,' said Doctor Extraordinary, sighing. 'It's Captain Chaos all right.'

'So this all looks very much like the work of Captain Chaos,' Lana Holliday was saying at the same time. 'And given what I've already told you about the doc, and the Q crystals, I think it's reasonable to assume that Chaos is still out there. She's obviously got help, and she's planning something big. Another attack. Wait a moment.' She squinted at the rows of text that were now appearing on her screen. 'Here's some of the panda's code. Phase Two, it says here.' She frowned. 'What's Phase Two?'

'Self-destructing in five seconds,' added the panda.

'Good idea to take cover at this point?' Sonny suggested.

231

'Because it –'

'**Three seconds**,' interrupted the panda.

'– is about to explode,' Sonny said as they all dived behind nearby workbenches.

There was a loud **PFFFT** kind of noise, and the panda exploded. (If you have a biscuit, eat it now.)

Right – back to that weapon that Spot noticed in the lab. Remember? The one that Lana thought was too powerful to use? The one that blasted a massive hole in the wall? *Wow*, you're probably thinking to yourself, *that sounds like a cool thing! What a shame it was only mentioned in passing and doesn't appear to have any relevance to the main story.*

Aha! Well, that's where you're wrong. We've pulled a classic author trick here, using a technique known as Barry's Badger. Want to know how it works so you can impress your teacher with your incredible knowledge of how stories are put together? OK, but this is just between us, right? It's a closely guarded author secret – so, if you want to know it, you must take the Author Vow of Secrecy. If you do, read on and take the vow. Otherwise, please close your eyes and skip to the next chapter, and no peeking. What's that? How will you know when it's the next chapter? Sorry, you're not in the Secret Author Gang so you're on your own here. *Scram.*

Right, that's got rid of them! If you are still reading, it means you want to know the top-secret author technique known as Barry's Badger, and you have agreed to take the Author Vow of Secrecy. Please get underneath your bedclothes and shout the following at the top of your voice:

I solemnly swear that I will not tell any non-authors about Barry's Badger!
If I do, I agree to be hit on the head with a large book until my socks fall off!

Right. You are now in the Secret Author Gang.

And here, just for you, is the tale of Barry's Badger.

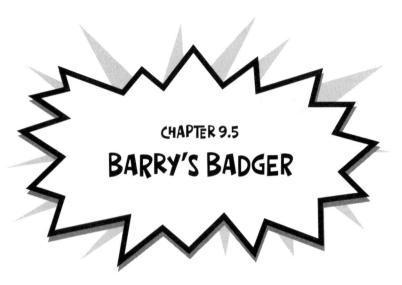

CHAPTER 9.5
BARRY'S BADGER

Once upon a time there was an extremely evil duck called Barry. He was bad-tempered, rude and sarcastic. Luckily, because of his lack of thumbs, he was unable to use social media, otherwise he would have been a real nightmare. But he still managed to make life pretty miserable for the other animals who lived in the same patch of dense forest as him – an area called Penguin Woods (we've no idea why). It was thousands of miles from the nearest wild penguin, and a good half-hour's drive from the nearest zoo penguin (whose name, although it's not relevant to this story, was Clive). But anyway, look, it was called Penguin Woods. It just was. Don't blame us – what are we, the Wood Name Police? Let's move on.

BARRY'S BADGER

One fine day in Penguin Woods . . . Look, we can tell you're not going to let this go. We know it's a stupid name for a patch of woodland, OK? But, if you keep interrupting and asking about it, we're never going to be able to get on with this story. Just go with it, right?

OK. One fine day in Penguin Woods, Barry the evil duck had gathered his whole gang together to plan a robbery of the local bakery, which – you're just going to have to take this one on the chin – was called Penguin Woods Bakery. Now Barry's gang was the nastiest, most villainous gang of animals you've ever seen. There was an owl called Knuckles – despite the fact that, being an owl, he didn't have any. There was also an extraordinarily badly behaved shrew whose name was Mrs Fepp, and two sisters, Nora and Brenda, who were both sheep. They weren't particularly evil, but every gang of villains needs muscle.

Anyway, on the day that story took place, Barry, Knuckles, Mrs Fepp, Nora and Brenda had all gathered 'neath a spreading oak tree at the very edge of Penguin Woods to plan their next heist.

'So here's the job,' quacked Barry in his deep, ducky

voice. 'We're gonna hit the Penguin Woods Bakery and steal all the bread.'

'Why we always gotta rob the bakery?' growled Knuckles.

'Yeah!' said Mrs Fepp, sharpening one of her claws on a stone. 'Why do we only steal bread? You're not even supposed to eat bread, Barry. It's bad for you. Says so on the sign by the pond.'

'Shut up,' snapped Barry, who (as we mentioned before) was very bad-tempered.

In any normal meeting, it's extremely poor practice to

snap 'shut up' at the other attendees, but he was an evil duck and had scant regard for maintaining good relations with his co-workers. Nora and Brenda gave bleats of agreement, being sheep and naturally averse to any kind of conflict.

At that point, a badger walked past, carrying a ladder over its shoulder. Nobody paid much attention to it because it didn't have any apparent relevance to the story. But it wandered past anyway, whistling a merry little badger tune, as the villainous animals simply carried on with their villainous animal plans.

'Why don't we rob a bank?' snarled Mrs Fepp. 'The Penguin Woods Bank is only round the corner, and it's run by field mice. Piece of cake. We go in there, distract them with cheese, and before they know it we've blasted our way into the vault and stolen all the acorns.'

(The animals of Penguin Woods use acorns as currency as they are unable to operate chip-and-PIN machines. It's quite ridiculous as acorns are freely available on the forest floor, so there's really no need for the field mice to gather them up and store them in a bank vault. But you know field mice: there's just no reasoning with them sometimes.)

'Yeah,' agreed Knuckles, spinning his head through 360 degrees just to show that he could. 'Then, with all them acorns, we can buy whatever we want.'

Barry the duck's eyes lit up with interest. 'Like what?' he asked. 'Bread?'

'What is it with you and bread?' asked Knuckles aggressively, regurgitating an owl pellet just to look cool. 'You're obsessed with flippin' bread. With all the acorns from the bank vault, you could buy, like, a private jet.'

'What's a duck gonna do with a private jet?' retorted

238

Barry, which seemed reasonable. 'Anyway,' he pointed out, 'I'm the head of this gang of criminals. And if I say we rob the bakery and steal all the bread then that's what we're gonna do. *Capeesh?*' (*Capeesh* is duck language for 'understand?' It's also sort of Italian but that's just a coincidence.)

'*Capeesh,*' said Knuckles and Mrs Fepp reluctantly (both of them had picked up a bit of duck language from hanging around with Barry for so long).

Brenda and Nora added a couple of *baas*, but nobody really cared; they wouldn't be needed unless things really kicked off, and they had to use their karate skills. (In fact, look, we may as well come clean here: Brenda and Nora are fairly incidental characters. They don't have any part to play; we just put them in to mess with the illustrator because sheep are kind of hard to draw. Oh, and by the way one of them was wearing a wizard's hat. And sunglasses. Sorry, Amy.)

All the other animals cowered in fear as Barry the duck and his crew of ne'er-do-wells cruised down the main street of Penguin Woods. Well, we say street. It was more of a long gap between the trees really, but you get the picture. Anyway, after a while, Barry, Knuckles, Mrs Fepp and the sheep who do not really feature in this story arrived at the Penguin Woods Bakery. Failing to notice the ladder propped up against the front wall, they rushed inside.

'Gimme all your bread, and be quick about it!' shouted Barry, brandishing the gun he'd been keeping in his pocket.

Yes, we know. Ducks don't have pockets. They also have wings, which are quite difficult to use to brandish anything, let alone a heavy gun. But go with it, OK? That part isn't important.

The vole behind the counter filled a large sack with bread, and Barry threw the sack over his shoulder – having returned the gun to his pocket – and led his gang of criminals back outside.

As Barry exited the bakery, a large badger fell off the roof directly on to his head, knocking him out cold. The other animals fled, even the sheep, and Barry was arrested by the Penguin Woods Police, who are all kingfishers, and put in jail. The badger, who had gone up on to the roof to clean out the gutters because it was a badger handyman, wandered off back into the forest, unaware that it had saved Penguin Woods from the scourge of Barry the duck for all time.

The End.

You're almost certainly now asking, 'Right, so what on earth was the point of all that?'

Well, we're about to tell you. You see, when the badger trotted past earlier in the story, it seemed like a completely random detail, didn't it? But it turned out to be important later on. And that, friends, is the technique known as Barry's Badger.

Here's the rule in brief in case you want to copy it out and memorize it:

If a badger appears in a story, then later on in that story it must fall off a roof and knock a duck unconscious. If it's not going to fall off a roof, it shouldn't be wandering about the woods with a ladder over its shoulder.

You're welcome.

CHAPTER 10

HERO DAY

Sonny and Spot were not the only people watching and listening as Professor Lana Holliday explained her theory about the Q crystals. Another pair of eyes was watching as she led them into the tent, and another pair of ears was listening as she told them how Doctor Extraordinary was still present as an echo in the universe because of the powers of this mysterious meteorite energy. The eyes that were watching were large and cute, and ringed with black fur. The ears were also black and fluffy. And they all belonged to the panda strapped into the pushchair.

When Spot and Sonny had chased after it in Paragon Park, the little robot had sent an emergency distress signal back to Castle Chaos, warning that it had entered pursuit mode and was taking evasive action. Immediately, PANDAmonium had put the feed from that particular panda up on her largest screen, and she and Captain Chaos had watched as it was wrestled into the pushchair and taken on the ferry.

'I knew that meddling Lana Holliday would get involved with this sooner or later,' said Captain Chaos crossly as the pushchair headed through the gates of Extraordinary HQ. 'She's bound to try and warn people about your stupid pandas.'

But as soon as Lana started her explanation she stopped grumbling and stared at the screen in amazement.

'Why are they messing about with an orange tent?' asked PANDAmonium. 'They have one of my precious pandas captive! This is no time for an indoor camping trip.'

'The tent shouldn't be your concern!' snapped Captain Chaos. 'Listen to what she's saying to those children!'

Lana could be heard from inside the tent talking about Q crystals and the effect they'd had on Doctor Extraordinary.

'It sounds boring,' said PANDAmonium. 'Just some science talk. She hasn't mentioned pandas once.'

'Not everything that isn't to do with pandas is boring,' Captain Chaos told her. 'Don't you get it? *Listen!*'

'Something about a shadow on the tent wall,' said PANDAmonium dismissively. 'Still no mention of pandas.' She was a brilliant scientist but, as we know, had no interest in anything unless it was panda-centric.

'She's talking about Extraordinary, you panda-obsessed fool!' Captain Chaos was running out of patience. 'He's back! Like me! Don't you understand? He's a ghost, too!'

'Well, why should that concern us?' PANDAmonium replied. 'He's a ghost, not a panda. And therefore I have no interest in him. Besides, he can't save Paragon City this time.' She gave an evil chuckle.

'Wait!' Captain Chaos held up a hand. 'They're explaining why not everyone can see him!'

Together they listened as Lana Holliday explained about Sonny tuning into the doc's ghost like an old-time radio trying to lock into a frequency.

'Ah, so that explains why you were the only person who

could see *me*!' the captain said. 'You must have been my number-one fan, too!'

'I certainly was not!' said PANDAmonium crossly. 'I just like a lot of the same things as you, that's all. Cats, for instance. And tea towels. And causing chaos. And the complete destruction of Paragon City.'

Captain Chaos was looking at her with a slight smile. 'Don't be embarrassed,' she said. 'It's rather touching.'

'Gah. Stop it!' said PANDAmonium, blushing. 'Anyway, let's focus here. We have an evil plan on the go! And perhaps you're right – even as a ghost, that meddling Doctor Extraordinary may try and stop me. The GIANT giant panda is nearly ready for the final mission. But until we launch let's keep the good doctor busy for a while, shall we? First thing tomorrow morning, I think it's time –' and here she gave a dramatic pause, so please halt your reading and count to seven – 'for Phase Two!'

The next day was Hero Day, when the citizens of Paragon City celebrated their hero, Doctor Extraordinary. All over the city, instead of their usual work clothes, people got out their superhero fancy-dress costumes and prepared for a day of street parties and celebrations leading up to a huge parade through the city.

This was set to be a Hero Day unlike any other, of course – and not just because of the impending panda attack. This would be the first time Hero Day had been celebrated without its, well, hero. But the mayor of the city had decreed that the parade should go ahead in memory of Doctor Extraordinary.

By this stage, there were robot pandas in homes all over Paragon City. Taken in by their cute appearance and even cuter squeaking noises, people had been happy to let them in. Their signature song-and-dance routine, the Panda Pop, was all over social media. Nobody suspected for a moment there was anything sinister about them, which in many ways was a pity because, as we know, there was.

On this particular Saturday morning, several of the pandas were actually being broadcast live on TV. They'd been assembled in the *Good Morning Paragon* studio for a fun item featuring the show's host, Susie Carpenter.

'Well, it's a very special day on *GMP* today,' she told the viewers. 'Of course – it's Hero Day! All over the city, people are putting on their fancy dress in preparation for the big parade.'

Susie herself, like everyone in the studio, was dressed as a superhero. But whereas most of the crew had made their own costumes she had badgered the TV station's wardrobe department into lending her a super-slick, professional costume, complete with high boots and a

silvery cape. Together with a glittery eye mask, she was confident she was in with a shout of winning the 'most like a real hero' award at the prize-giving in the park later.

'Now,' she said, giving a slight twirl so that her cape billowed out behind her in a cool fashion, 'this year we might not have actual Doctor Extraordinary to take part in the parade, but we do have a lot of very special visitors to our city. If your family's anything like mine, your kids will have been completely obsessed with the small pandas that have appeared all over town this week. My social media feeds are completely full of it – if you follow me online, you'll have even seen me having a go at the dance, ha ha!'

She threw back her hair and laughed. 'It's the craze that's captured the whole of Paragon City, from the corridors of our high schools to the chambers of City Hall. In fact, have a look at this! Even the mayor's been getting her Panda Pop on!'

The picture cut to a grainy piece of footage shot on a phone. The mayor of Paragon City – a tall woman in red robes – was giving a speech behind a podium on the steps of the large stone City Hall.

'I know everyone's concerned about the recent rise in crime,' said the mayor, whose name was Lucinda Klopp, 'but I'd still like you to show your faith in me by giving me your vote in the upcoming elections. In fact –' she stepped out from behind the lectern and began to jig unconvincingly backwards and forwards, rotating her arms like the pistons of a malfunctioning steam train and chanting to the tune of the Panda Pop – 'vote Lucinda Klopp, vote Lucinda Klopp.'

Behind her, one of her assistants could be seen burying his head in his hands with embarrassment.

'Wasn't that something?' said Susie Carpenter with a thin, patronizing smile as the camera cut back to her. 'Well, let's see if we can do a little better, shall we? Because live with me here in the studio, for a special Hero Day treat, are several of the pandas that our team have been rounding up. And so we can all be "down with the kids", as they say nowadays, we're going to have a little Panda Pop lesson right here in the studio! This should be interesting. I'm sure I'll be terrible at it!' (She knew she wouldn't be because she'd spent the last week having private lessons with a dance teacher, but she'd read that self-deprecation goes down well with the viewing public.)

Before long, Susie Carpenter and no fewer than six of the robot pandas were gyrating round the studio floor.

'Ooh, we're just like one of those boy bands, aren't we?' she said. 'Only with pandas. A boy pand! Ha ha!'

On either side of her, the pandas squeaked out their cute little song and danced their cute little dance, until something rather unexpected happened.

At that exact moment, out in the middle of the Shadow Mountains, in the very heart of Castle Chaos, PANDAmonium unleashed the next phase of her plan.

'It's time for a big, bananas, bear-based bonanza of badness!' she cried as she strode over to the main panda control panel.

Opening a clear plastic cover, she hovered her finger dramatically over the switch labelled **Phase Two**. She'd been preparing for this moment for some time and had a series of witty remarks prepared.

'It's time to unleash a panda-demic!'

Captain Chaos looked puzzled. 'Isn't that what we've done already?' she asked.

PANDAmonium ignored her. She'd been thinking up cool panda-based things to say for days now, and she didn't want her big scene spoiled with logic.

'Yes, well.' She collected herself with some difficulty. 'It's time for the panda-demic to become even more . . . infectious. Time to expand-a the panda-demic!'

'Again . . .' began Captain Chaos.

'Shut up!' said PANDAmonium between clenched teeth. 'Honestly, you've been the main villain for years and years. Can't you let me have just this one villainous moment without ruining it?'

'Sorry.' Captain Chaos held up her hands in apology. After all, she was a ghost and in many ways completely powerless. She wasn't going to be able to invade Paragon City without help, even if it was from a completely panda-obsessed maniac. In those circumstances, it's very important to keep your sidekick onside, so to speak.

'Do go on,' she said with fake politeness.

PANDAmonium took a moment to gather her thoughts, still with her finger poised over the switch. 'Right,' she said. 'It's time to unleash a panda-demic. No, wait, I've done that one, haven't I?'

She scrabbled in her pocket for a crumpled piece of paper on which she'd jotted down some extra villain quips, just in case. And if you're wondering whether the paper was made out of bamboo – it was.

'Ah yes,' she said, squinting a little to read her own spidery handwriting. 'It's time to execute the plan-da, expand-a my panda propaganda and force their hand-a to give into my demands-a. And I shall shout this from the veranda. In Uganda. With Amanda.'

'Totally off her rocker,' muttered Captain Chaos to herself, but not loudly enough to be heard.

At that point, PANDAmonium – whose list of things that rhyme with panda had finally come to an end-a – flicked down the switch.

'So?' Captain Chaos rubbed her hands together excitedly, looking out of the large window in the direction of Paragon City in case she suddenly saw a huge explosion or at least a plume of smoke. 'What actually is Phase Two? Was it the laser eyes? Are they all going to explode? Or are they melding together into one enormous, destructive, multi-headed hydra-panda?'

'A multi-headed hydra-panda?' said PANDAmonium

scornfully. 'Don't be ridiculous. Our next move is to invade the city with a GIANT giant panda robot, remember? What would be the point of softening them up with a second GIANT giant panda? Try and concentrate!'

Again keeping her temper with some difficulty, Captain Chaos asked, 'So what are the robot pandas doing, then?'

'Oh!' PANDAmonium's eyes sparkled with glee. 'The question is what *aren't* they doing. You see –' another villainous chuckle escaped her lips – 'the thing people don't know about pandas is that they do like a laugh.'

'Do they?'

'Oh yes. Pandas have an extraordinarily good sense of humour. In fact, they're jokers. Practical jokers.'

Captain Chaos's shoulders dropped, visions of destructive laser-eyed pandas evaporating from her imagination. 'So, what?' she asked. 'They're just going to play jokes on people? Like leaving banana skins in the street or something?'

'Oooh, good one!' PANDAmonium rushed to a keyboard and started tapping furiously. 'I'll add that to the algorithm.'

'Give me strength,' said Captain Chaos with a sigh, burying her face in her hands.

Back in the *Good Morning Paragon* TV studio, something very strange happened to the pandas that had been busily and sweetly performing a synchronized dance routine, lined up on either side of Susie Carpenter. As PANDAmonium finally finished her puns and flicked her switch, there was a whining noise from all the robots, and small silver horns burst out of the top of their heads, just between their ears. At once, the pandas stopped being cute and their dancing ceased immediately.

They started to run riot around the TV studio, chewing on the furniture and pushing over the decorative pot plants that were scattered artfully about.

'Oh!' Susie gasped as a panda climbed up her leg with surprising speed and started chomping on her carefully arranged superhero mask. 'Well, I'm not quite sure what's going . . . Get off!' Another panda had stolen one of her boots and disappeared behind the sofa with it.

'*SUSIE!*' The producer was screaming in her ear. 'Say something! Say something *sensible*!'

'Ooh, you cheeky little scamp!' said Susie, giving a very fake-sounding laugh and attempting to disentangle the panda's teeth from her hair. 'Well, they do say never work with children or animals . . . ha. Ha ha. Ha. Ha.'

She laughed unconvincingly and hopped over to the sofa, still with one of the pandas clinging to her neck, to search for the boot from her hero costume. But the panda who'd taken it had already reduced it to shreds. This was a severe test of Susie Carpenter's patience – they were extremely nice boots, and she was never going to win anything at the prize ceremony with one bare foot.

'Can you just STOP IT!' she yelled, her temper suddenly snapping as a third panda attempted to take her other boot. 'BOG OFF!' She kicked out at it furiously.

'*Don't kick the pandas!*' shrieked the panicked producer in her earpiece. 'Kicking pandas is BAD TV, Susie. *BAAAAD TV!* No kicking!'

But Susie wasn't listening. By now, the pandas had all started emitting an irritating high-pitched hum, like the noise you do in class to annoy the supply teacher.

WHEEEEEEEEE! went the pandas as three of them ganged up in a fresh attempt to get Susie's other boot.

'No!' she said scolding them, hopping backwards ineffectually. 'Get away!'

'No panda-kicking, remember!' bellowed the producer, but it was too late.

Susie lashed out with her foot, connecting with the middle panda. She had been a star rugby player before she became a TV presenter, and so, as you'd expect, it was a good kick. The panda sailed through the air directly into the camera, knocking it over backwards.

The last thing that viewers of *Good Morning Paragon* saw before the transmission was cut was one of the other pandas, which had climbed up into the lights suspended from the ceiling, biting a cable in half and causing a shower of sparks to rain down on the studio. Just before the picture dissolved into static, the panda looked directly into the camera, its eyes now glowing an eerie red colour, and waved its paws in an expression of evil triumph.

Sonny, who was watching this over the breakfast table as usual, let out a yelp of shock. 'Doc!' he shouted. 'It's started! The pandas have gone evil!'

Doctor Extraordinary came rushing in through the wall. 'I knew it!' he said tensely, watching the pandas steal Susie Carpenter's boot live on-screen. 'This is some scheme of Captain Chaos's! Not sure why she's using pandas, though. She's never cooked up a panda-based plot before.'

'Never mind that now!' Sonny fumbled for his phone, thumbing frantically for Spot's number. 'We've got to be ready for action! Nobody else has worked out she's back! We need to warn somebody!'

Back at Castle Chaos, PANDAmonium was jumping around in delight as she watched the live feeds coming in from her robot pandas. It wasn't just in the TV studio – they had all turned evil and started causing chaos across the city.

'Yes!' she was cackling, watching footage of Paragonians, most of them in fancy dress ready for Hero Day, vainly attempting to fight them off. 'Cause havoc, my little monochrome beauties! My devilish little fuzz moppets!'

'*Fuzz moppets?*' Captain Chaos frowned at this, but she

was unable to hold back a grudging sense of admiration. The tiny pandas were causing mayhem and destruction all over the place. 'They do seem to be stealing a lot of people's shoes,' she said, squinting at the screens.

'Ha *haaa*, yes!' said PANDAmonium, her eyes shining with triumph. 'That is the most evil part of my plan! I have instructed my devil pandas to target shoes wherever possible. A population without shoes is a population without hope! Without them, the people of Paragon City will be powerless!' She cackled once again.

'Well, they'll certainly be shoeless,' pointed out Captain Chaos.

But she decided not to pursue it further. Or per-*shoe* it, if you like. PANDAmonium's plot may have been deranged, and unduly centred on pandas and shoes, but Captain Chaos had to admit she was impressed by it. After all, you couldn't deny that it was causing chaos. And that – as her name would suggest – was Captain Chaos's favourite thing.

CHAPTER 11
ATTACK OF THE GIANT GIANT PANDA

Responding to a frantic phone call from Sonny, Spot abandoned her own breakfast and ran through the city towards his block of flats. By now, Paragon City was in complete chaos.

'*Wheeeeeeee!*' shrieked a panda as it zip-lined down a power cable, raining sparks on to the street below.

Spot, pen clamped firmly between her teeth as usual, ducked and dived down the road, avoiding the mayhem on either side as she desperately tried to make her way to Sonny's flat. Pandas were pushing over bins and chasing dogs down the pavement. Two of them had somehow got hold of a car and were driving it wildly down the road, one crouched on the floor, operating the pedals, while the other clung to the steering wheel. People in superhero fancy dress were fleeing in terror. It was, quite literally, panda pandamonium.

'And to top it all, I think it's started raining,' muttered Spot, crossly blowing her wet hair out of her face as she was suddenly drenched by a deluge of chilly water.

But it wasn't raining. A group of the rogue panda robots had pushed over a fire hydrant nearby, sending a powerful jet of water high into the air.

Here and there, Spot could see more fancy-dress-clad citizens running along the pavements in panic, many of them with home-made capes trailing behind them and most of them without at least one of their shoes. The city was filled with cries of alarm, car alarms, sirens and high-pitched squeaking as the pandas went about their mischievous business.

'Who will save us?' wailed one woman as she dashed past.

'That,' replied Spot, dodging a panda that was skateboarding directly towards her, holding a lit firework, 'is exactly what I'm on my way to find out.'

PANDAmonium was ecstatic. '*Yesssss*,' she said, rubbing her hands together and cackling. 'Wreak havoc, my black-and-white beauties! Make the city suffer!'

On the large screen was a patchwork of different shots of panda-based mayhem. Captain Chaos stood beside her, hopping impatiently from foot to foot.

'Is it time to launch the main attack?' she asked impatiently. 'Surely that's enough low-grade bear business for now?'

'*Low-grade bear business?*' PANDAmonium placed a hand on her chest in a gesture of wounded pride. 'How dare you! My precious cubs have reduced Paragon City to a total madhouse! After years of that tight-costumed fool looking after them constantly, the Paragonians are no longer capable of defending themselves! Our secret weapon will meet with no resistance!'

'Yes, yes,' said Captain Chaos, 'it's very impressive. But isn't it time for the giant robot? That's my favourite part – the giant robot bit.'

'Oh, very well.'

PANDAmonium reluctantly tore her gaze away from the screen and moved to a large control panel at one side of the lair. She pressed a button and spoke into a small microphone that stuck out on a metal stalk.

'ACTIVATE THE GIANT GIANT PANDA!' she said in a loud, strident voice.

'I wanted to say that,' said Captain Chaos, complaining. 'That's the best line.'

'Say it, then,' snapped PANDAmonium.

'Well, there's no point now, is there?' Captain Chaos said sulkily. 'You've already done it.'

'Plus,' PANDAmonium pointed out, 'you're a ghost, so nobody except me would be able to hear you.'

'Being a ghost is rubbish,' muttered Captain Chaos

as she followed her sidekick towards the main doors of Castle Chaos.

Outside, the mountains stretched away to the east, with Paragon City dimly visible in the distance through a gap between two of the peaks. As Captain Chaos and PANDAmonium came out of the doors, there was a deep rumbling from underground. Several small boulders were dislodged from the nearby hillside and went skittering down into the valley and splashed into the tranquil mountain lake that was not far away from the castle entrance.

'Prepare yourself!' said PANDAmonium dramatically. 'My greatest creation is about to be unleashed!'

She pulled a control unit from her belt and pressed a button. At once, the waters of the mountain lake began to ripple. Small waves started lapping at the shore. The disturbance grew, and before long the water was boiling like a kettle.

'Was it really necessary to have your creation appear dramatically from underneath the lake?' asked Captain Chaos rather irritably. 'You could have just brought it out of the main doors.'

'That's why I make a far better supervillain than

you,' said PANDAmonium. 'I have the necessary eye for theatre.'

Slowly, a gigantic shape was rising out of the lake. With a grinding of underwater machinery and a bubbling and splashing of greenish water, a platform was gradually being raised. And on top of that platform was a huge robot panda, the size of a house. And not a small house either. One of those houses you drive past and go, 'Ooh, that's a big house. I wonder who lives there.'

'ACTIVATE THE GIANT GIANT PANDA!' bellowed PANDAmonium again. It was such an impressive thing to shout that she'd decided to shout it no fewer than three times during this process, which she'd been planning for some time.

The panda's eyes lit up like headlamps, and it lumbered to the lakeshore with a crashing and clanging of its gigantic metal feet. A hatch opened in its back, and the two villains climbed in, using a ladder that had been specially built on one side of its tail. Once inside, PANDAmonium led the way to the control room, which was a glass bubble sticking out on top of the panda's head, just between its ears. Taking her place in one of

the two pilot's chairs, she pressed a large button, yelling, 'ACTIVATE THE GIANT GIANT PANDA!' for the third and final time.

'There's no need to keep saying that,' grumbled Captain Chaos, who wasn't enjoying this giant-robot attack nearly as much as the ones where she'd been on her own. 'It's very much already been activated. And you were pressing the button anyway.'

Holding up a finger for silence, PANDAmonium broke into a smile of triumph as the panda began to walk ponderously forward, heading down the rough mountain track towards the distant skyscrapers of Paragon City.

'Finally,' she said, her eyes glittering cruelly, 'it's time for a proper attack. This is going to be fun . . . In fact, you could say it's going to be an absolute blast.'

Captain Chaos looked at her with a worried frown as she broke into peals of crazed laughter.

Always on the lookout for a good story, roving reporter Ben Bailey had rushed to Paragon City Police HQ. With his camera operator trailing after him, he raced through reception, which was full of panicking police officers, most of them being menaced by pandas in a variety of ways that you'll have to imagine for yourself because we need to get on with the story. It was so chaotic that nobody stopped him as he continued down a corridor and into the main control room.

'Make sure you get this!' he shouted over his shoulder to the camera operator as he shoved open the door and edged inside.

Every single phone in the large, cluttered room was

ringing frantically as more members of the PCPD dashed to and fro like wasps escaping from a kicked bin.

'What's going on out there?' wailed one officer, shaking her leg frantically to try and dislodge a panda that was attempting to steal her shoe.

'I'm going to lock myself in the cells until it's all over!' yelled another, a tall, thin man carrying a large bunch of keys who shoved his way past Ben and disappeared, jangling, down a staircase.

'Scenes of *complete chaos* here at Paragon City Police HQ,' said Ben into the camera. 'If the people of the city were hoping for a hero to rescue them, then it's clear that he or she is not going to be wearing a police uniform. Because, well, they're either freaking out or locking themselves away. This is Ben Bailey, reporting live on the unfolding scenes as the pandas take over Paragon.'

That was a good line, he thought to himself. He'd make sure that was posted on benbaileynews.com as soon as possible.

'It's *complete chaos* out there!' Spot burst through the front door to find Sonny and Doctor Extraordinary glued to the window, looking in horror at the unfolding scene below them. Officer Dusty was sitting at the table, holding a bowl of cereal, watching TV with an expression of frozen shock. The sound was turned down, but the screen showed Ben Bailey's excited face as he reported from the police HQ building.

'You made it!' said Sonny. 'Thank goodness!'

'We never thought the evil plot would start so soon!' said Doctor Extraordinary. 'We need to act fast!'

'What . . .' Officer Dusty spoke quietly, eyes fixed on the screen. 'What's going on? What is this?'

'See if you can talk to him, will you?' Sonny asked Spot. 'We've been trying to get him to warn the police department that it's a Captain Chaos attack, but he just can't seem to take it in.'

'Officer Nelson?' said Spot gently, sitting down opposite him at the table. 'It's Spot here. Hello. We need to tell you something really important.'

Dusty simply stared at her. After weeks of night shifts battling a crime wave, this sudden attack seemed to have completely shut down his brain.

'Dad!' Sonny came to join Spot at the table. 'It's really,

really important! You have to listen to us!'

'It's *complete chaos*.' Sonny's dad pointed to the TV screen with a trembling spoon, milk dripping off the end and on to the tablecloth. 'Those pandas have gone completely mad! They're attacking everyone! Look, that one's stolen somebody's shoe!'

'Yes, Dad, we know.' Sonny turned to Spot with an expression of helplessness.

'I remember this from one of Mum's psychology textbooks,' she told him quietly. 'He's completely unable to deal with what's happening. He's in shock.'

'But we need to warn the police department that it's Captain Chaos!' yelled Sonny. His dad turned to him with a frown.

'But . . . she got blown up,' he said in a faint, puzzled voice.

Over by the window, Doctor Extraordinary had been getting increasingly agitated. The wide avenue below was filled with the sound of smashing glass, car alarms and the shrieks of fleeing people.

'We don't have time for this,' he said to Sonny and Spot tensely.

Sonny looked at his father. 'Dad,' he said urgently, 'the city's under attack. It's time to be a hero.'

'I'm no hero,' Officer Dusty said sadly.

His gaze roved round the room before landing sadly on the open door of his son's bedroom. He gestured vaguely towards the posters and memorabilia that plastered the walls.

'*He's* your hero. Not me.'

Sonny felt these words like a hammer blow. It suddenly dawned on him that all this time he'd been idolizing Doctor Extraordinary, his dad had just assumed he was coming in second best.

'That's not how it is at all,' he said gently. 'You're right. The city needs a hero. But I'm asking *you* to be that hero, Dad. That's all I've ever wanted.'

There was a moment of silence. Sonny's dad shifted uncomfortably in his chair, looking for a split second as if he was going to get up from the table. But then he glanced once again at the TV, which was showing more shots of the panda robots running riot.

'I'm sorry, son,' he said, his shoulders slumping. 'I know you want a hero. But that's just not me. I'm no match

for . . . whatever this is. I'm just a cop.'

'Fine!' shouted Sonny furiously, pushing back his chair and getting up from the table. 'Come on, Spot. We're obviously not going to get any help here.'

'Where are you going?' asked his dad as they dashed for the door.

'We're going to do what you refuse to do!' replied his son. 'We're going to try and save Paragon City!'

Sonny's dad buried his head in his hands as the door slammed shut behind them.

Fearless roving reporter Ben Bailey had covered many exciting news stories in the course of his career. He'd covered many weird news stories as well. But nothing quite as weird or exciting as this.

'As you can see, Susie, the pandas are now causing widespread devastation right across Paragon City,' he said to the camera.

Behind him, a small ornamental garden was visible. But now, pandas had pulled up all the trees and shrubs, and one of them was eating the flowers. Ben moved to one side, and his camera operator followed.

'The Paragon City Police Department have issued a statement. They say that, in the absence of Doctor Extraordinary, they are not in a position to deal with the situation, and they're advising everyone to stay in their homes. In fact, if you look down the street,' he said, 'you can see that there are pandas everywhere. It's . . . Get off!

He started hopping sideways, shaking his left leg to reveal that a panda was stealing his shoe. Another climbed on to his head and started rubbing flowers in his hair.

Sonny, Spot and Doctor Extraordinary stood on the edge of the crowd that had gathered, watching this strange scene unfold. Several hundred people in superhero fancy dress had begun to congregate round the news crew, apparently hoping for some kind of guidance. But, having rushed down the road towards them full of purpose, Sonny now found himself with no idea whatsoever what to do next.

'Go on, then,' said Spot. 'This is the bit where we, you know, save the city. Remember?'

'Yeah.' Sonny shuffled his feet awkwardly, looking at the crowd and the bright lights attached to the top of the TV cameras and feeling approximately three millimetres tall. 'Maybe I'm not the right person to save Paragon City after all. Now I'm actually here, it's kind of overwhelming.'

He turned to Doctor Extraordinary and looked the ghost straight in the face. 'I'm not sure I can do this,' he told him frankly. 'I don't think I can be the hero. A hero wouldn't be this terrified.'

The doc looked down at Sonny kindly. 'Want to know a real piece of behind-the-scenes superhero information?'

he asked. Sonny nodded. 'If you're not terrified, you're not doing it right,' he went on. 'Because nothing's really worth doing if it doesn't scare you, even just a little bit.'

'This scares me really quite a lot,' said Sonny shakily.

'Well then, that means it must be really, really worth doing,' said Doctor Extraordinary. 'I always used to think: the bigger the task, the greater the hero.'

'You really think I can be a hero?'

'You already are,' declared the doc. 'The only one who believed in me enough to see me. And the only one who cares enough about this city to try and do something about it. I can't think of a better person to carry on my legacy.'

'Right.' Sonny squared his shoulders, and Spot gave him an encouraging pat on the back. 'Let's do this. Because if I can be a hero, we all can.'

Together he and Spot raced forward to stand beside Ben Bailey. Spot grabbed the panda that had been worrying at his shoe, and, lifting it up like a naughty toddler, she threw it into a nearby bin. (Note: do not do this with actual toddlers, not even the naughty ones.) Meanwhile, Sonny swatted at the panda on Ben's head, eventually dislodging

277

it, at which point it fell to the ground with a clang.

'Don't stay in your homes!' yelled Sonny into the camera. 'It's up to us! This is our city, and we've got to save it! What would Doctor Extraordinary do?'

'I'd save Paragon City, of course!' replied the doc, who was standing beside him – not that anybody else could see. Or hear, for that matter.

'He'd save Paragon City!' echoed Sonny. 'But the doc can't help us right now. So we've all got to turn into heroes instead. Come on, then! Help us! They're only pandas, after all! Let's take our city back!'

Ben Bailey listened to this very stirring speech with a dawning expression of excitement. 'You know what, *GMP* viewers?' he said. 'This kid is exactly right! We let these pandas into our homes. And – dammit! – into our hearts. But now they've turned on us. It's time to take a stand! And say *no, you CAN'T have my shoe!*'

One of the pandas had crawled back towards his leg, but now Ben lashed out with his foot. The kick connected well, and the panda rolled away down the street, coming to rest against a parked car with a satisfying clank.

'See!' said Spot, joining Sonny, her face flushed and

excited. 'We can all be heroes! Rise up and defend your city!'

'As Doctor Extraordinary would say,' shouted Sonny, catching the doc's eye and grinning, 'why be ordinary when you can be *extraordinary*!'

To his delight, he could hear cheering from some of the nearby windows where people were watching the live broadcast.

'Onward to the unknown!' yelled Sonny, and the cheering intensified.

In the crowd, he saw a woman dressed in a leotard and a long purple cape that looked suspiciously like a bath towel grab another of the red-eyed, evil pandas and attempt to shove it into a large metal bin on the pavement.

'Come on!' she told the people nearby. 'The kid's right! We've got to stop these furry little fiends! All of us! Let's go!'

And the cheers grew louder still.

'What are they cheering about?' asked Sonny's dad edgily, hearing the noise through Miss Abigail's window. Since Sonny had left he'd felt as if he was balanced on a knife edge, desperate to do something but unable to work out where to start. In search of company and – if he was honest – advice, he'd wandered down the corridor and found the old lady sitting in her window with her patchwork quilt bunched up on her lap.

'I think they're cheering for the city's heroes,' said Miss Abigail mildly.

Officer Dusty grunted. 'And who might they be?' he asked grumpily. 'Not me anyway,' he added to himself, peering down at the street below.

'Oh, I don't know,' she replied softly. 'Help me with this, would you?'

She lifted the corners of the quilt, struggling to shake out the heavy folds of material.

'You've never finished it?' said Dusty, turning back from the window in excitement to help her.

'Well, a job like this is never really finished,' said Miss Abigail. 'See?'

Dusty, who had been pulling the other two corners away from her to flatten out the material, turned, and his eyes widened in surprise and delight. For the first time, he got a proper look at what she'd been sewing. Picked out in intricate detail was a gigantic patchwork of Paragon City itself. Tiny skyscrapers had been embroidered on to the brown and grey squares in the middle. Islands and boats decorated the blue squares on the right that made up Sunrise Lake. And, to the left, browns and greens showed the expanse of the Shadow Mountains.

'A city's made up of lots of different parts,' Miss Abigail told Dusty kindly. 'And every one of these stitches is important. Just because you don't have your own island –' with a wrinkled finger she pointed to the green '*e*' of Extraordinary Island, far out in the cloth lake – 'it doesn't mean that your part in the whole quilt isn't a vital one.'

'I wish you could show Sonny this,' said Dusty sadly. 'I think he's only interested in one hero.'

'Well . . .' Miss Abigail turned once again to look out of the window. 'Why don't you go and show him how wrong he is?'

With a thudding of feet and a clanking of gears, the GIANT giant panda climbed down the final foothill of the Shadow Mountains. From the control room on the

top of its head, Captain Chaos could now see the vast jumble of buildings and parkland that made up Paragon City, filling the landscape up to the shores of the glittering lake. Thin columns of smoke rose here and there, and even from this distance she could hear the shouts and screams as people began their fightback against the panda invasion.

'Those fools,' PANDAmonium said scornfully from her pilot's chair. 'They're so busy fighting off my little fuzz moppets, they don't even see the real threat coming.'

'Indeed,' Captain Chaos said. 'We'll be able to cause a huge amount of damage.'

'Well, yes.' PANDAmonium

282

looked at her in surprise. 'Maximum damage.'

There was a slight pause as the giant bear continued lumbering forward, now tilting down the final slope and heading into the city.

'Sorry,' said Captain Chaos finally. 'But when you say "maximum damage" . . . what do you mean exactly?'

'The total destruction of Paragon City, of course,' her former sidekick replied.

'Because I thought the plan was to drive this panda robot into the city and smash things up a bit. Like we usually do,' said the captain. 'Then we get defeated, and we say, "You may have stopped us this time, but we'll be back," yadda yadda yadda, and off to the castle for tea. Right?'

'Things have changed now that I'm in charge,' said PANDAmonium with a cruel grin. 'I've made some special modifications to this latest robot.'

'Not another self-destruct system, is it?' Captain Chaos nervously scanned the control panel for a big red button.

'Oh no,' said PANDAmonium, laughing. 'This causes much more trouble. You see, this entire GIANT giant panda is, in fact, a GIANT giant bomb powered by Q energy.

283

And, when it reaches the Q crystals in the centre of Paragon Park, it will create a GIANT giant bang.'

'What?' Captain Chaos looked at her in horror. 'Are you completely out of your mind?'

'Yes.' PANDAmonium seemed startled that her former boss even needed to ask the question. 'Of course I am. I've created my own personal army of robot pandas, plus an extra giant robot panda that is in fact a huge panda bomb. Of course I'm completely out of my mind. And I'm about to wipe Paragon City from the surface of the planet once and for all.'

'But, but . . .' Captain Chaos felt a chill down her back. (And considering she was a ghost that was fairly impressive.) 'That wasn't the plan!'

'It might not have been *your* plan, but it is mine. A proper evil one for once.'

'But if you completely wipe out Paragon City,' said Captain Chaos, 'there won't be anything left to attack! We'll have nothing to do!'

'Well, we'll just go and blow something else up, then,' said PANDAmonium airily. 'There's loads of cities –

they're all over the place. You've got New Chesterton, Bridge Heights, Lakeview, Skyville . . . We can blow them all up.'

Captain Chaos looked round the control room in alarm. Despite constantly attacking it, the complete and utter destruction of Paragon City had never been her aim. In fact, the thought of the huge smouldering crater that would soon be replacing the buildings ahead of her filled her with sadness and horror. She realized that, for the first time in many years, she was going to do something she had never considered. She was going to ask Doctor Extraordinary for help.

'Hey! Wait! Where do you think you're going?' cried PANDAmonium as Captain Chaos disappeared through the wall and set off towards Paragon City as fast as her ghostly legs would carry her.

CHAPTER 12
THE SPIRIT OF DOCTOR EXTRAORDINARY

Sonny Nelson had never considered himself to be a particularly inspiring person. He felt that saving the day was very much something other people did. Not his dad and the largely ineffectual Paragon City Police Department. And certainly not him, Doctor Extraordinary's number-one fan. In fact, for most of his life, Sonny had been so obsessed with finding out any details he could about the superhero that he'd almost forgotten to find out any details about himself. But over the last couple of weeks that had changed gradually and very subtly.

Sonny had realized that he was no longer simply a

follower. His friend Spot, and even Doctor Extraordinary himself, now looked to him for leadership. A couple of months ago, Sonny would never have dreamed of making a rousing speech live on TV. But now he'd done so, and he and his friends quickly began to realize that a lot of people had been watching, and, what's more, they had taken his speech very much to heart.

All over the city, Paragonians began fighting back against the robot pandas. Grabbing any weapons they could, they started to drive the evil creatures out of their homes, and in many cases managed to recover their stolen shoes.

Sonny and Spot were continuing their battle against the pandas in the wide central street that led towards Paragon Park. Ben Bailey had now joined the fight, too, wielding a large fluffy microphone like a sword. And he wasn't the only one ready to lend a hand.

To his delight, Sonny heard sirens behind them, and turned to see several police cars speeding up the road. A familiar figure was leaning dangerously out of the passenger window of the first car, waving his hands frantically.

'Sonny!' yelled Officer Dusty Nelson as the vehicles screeched to a stop. 'I'm sorry! You were right! I've rounded up my squad, and we're here to help!'

'Hey, Dad,' said Sonny, attempting to sound all cool and hero-like, but giving himself away by wiping his eyes. 'Good to see you.'

He was immediately pulled into a huge hug by his father before they stepped back and looked at each other.

'You were right all along, son,' his dad told him. 'It's up to us now. Paragon City's worth saving. And if we work together we can *all* save it.'

As he spoke those last words, Sonny's father squinted curiously at the empty patch of street behind his son. He could make out a strange haze in the air and, as he watched, it thickened until he could clearly see a familiar figure standing there, looking at him proudly.

'Hey!' he said. 'It's Doctor Extraordinary!'

'What?' Sonny exclaimed. 'You can see him?'

'What?' exclaimed the doc at exactly the same time. 'You can see me?'

'Remember what Professor Holliday said?' said Spot excitedly. 'She thought you were able to see the doc because you were kind of tuned into the right wavelength. Maybe that was the right wavelength all along – just wanting to save Paragon City!'

'That's what we're here for, right?' Officer Dusty asked the doc, who grinned and raised a thumb in reply. 'So . . . what's the plan?'

'Get rid of these annoying pandas!' Sonny replied. 'Help the people of Paragon take back their city!'

'You got it!' His dad beckoned to his fellow officers. 'You heard him! Paragon City Police Department . . . as they say in the business: let's go kick some panda butt!'

With a roar, the officers surged forward, sending several pandas scurrying away towards the park, squeaking with alarm. And, as the police department was finally able to step up and fight for their city, more and more of them found that they could see the semi-transparent figure who ran alongside them, his face bright with excitement as Doctor Extraordinary joined in the battle to save his beloved city.

Before long, the pandas were in full retreat, streaming north up the wide avenue towards the park, with the citizens of Paragon City, led by their police force, in hot

pursuit. Sonny and Spot were racing to keep up, whooping and cheering in triumph as they sprinted along. But before they reached the park they stopped in their tracks. A figure in brightly coloured clothes was approaching down a side street, waving its arms frantically.

Doctor Extraordinary looked at her in alarm. 'It's her!

It's Captain Chaos! Come on!'

He led Sonny and Spot away from the charging crowd and halted in front of his arch-enemy.

'Well, well, well. Captain Chaos. I should have known you'd be behind the panda invasion. Looks like you've been defeated once again.'

'It's not me!' said Captain Chaos. 'Well, it kind of is me, to be fair. But also it isn't! It's my sidekick! Well, not quite my sidekick any more. Since I've been a ghost, she's kind of become the main kick. Remember my chief scientist?'

'Anna Podium?' asked the doc. 'The one who used to invent all the giant robots? The one who went completely loopy and made that self-destruct system that sealed us inside the control room?'

'That's her, yes,' said Captain Chaos.

'The one who was, in fact, directly responsible for both of us getting blown up?'

'Yup.'

'In that case, yes, I'm familiar with her work.'

'Well, she's now calling herself PANDAmonium!' explained the captain. 'And if you thought she was mad before – well, she's even madder now. And completely obsessed with pandas. It's her who sent all these robots to invade the city!'

'As you can see, her villainous plan has failed.' Doctor Extraordinary dusted his hands together in a satisfied fashion. 'Thanks to my young friends here, Sonny and Spot, and the good people of the Paragon City Police

Department, the city has been saved! All without me lifting a finger. Not that anybody would have seen if I had lifted a finger, of course, as I'm a ghost. Just like you, in fact. How are you finding it? Kind of annoying, isn't it?'

'*So* annoying!' replied Captain Chaos, forgetting the danger for a second and just feeling glad to have someone to chat to about the frustrations of being a ghost. 'You just can't get anything done, can you? No superpowers any more. Nobody can see or hear you. Frankly, it's completely rubbish.'

'I really miss biscuits,' said Doctor Extraordinary wistfully. 'I'd love a biscuit right now.'

'Ooh yes, biscuits,' agreed Captain Chaos with a faraway look in her eye. 'Nothing better than a nice choccy bicky when you're plotting to attack Paragon City. Ah, which reminds me!' She clicked her ghostly fingers silently. 'That's what I came to tell you! The small pandas are just a distraction! PANDAmonium's mounting the main attack right now, and you've got to help me stop her!'

'And what is the main attack?' asked Sonny, heading off

any more possible chat about biscuits. Ghosts get easily sidetracked, he was discovering.

'It'll be a giant robot,' said Doctor Extraordinary casually. 'It's always a giant robot.'

'It *is* a giant robot,' confirmed Captain Chaos. 'A giant panda, to be exact.'

'A GIANT giant panda, in fact,' said Spot smugly before Sonny shushed her. Something in Captain Chaos's expression was telling him there was no time to lose.

'She's made the entire robot into a bomb!' the supervillain said. 'It's powered by Q energy – so she needs the crystals in the Doctor Extraordinary Museum to set it off. As soon as the GIANT giant panda reaches the crystals it'll explode and destroy the whole of Paragon City!'

There was a brief pause as they all took this news in. 'But that's completely absurd!' said Doctor Extraordinary in horror. 'Destroy the whole city? That's monstrous!'

'I didn't know what she was planning, honest!' said Captain Chaos pleadingly. 'I was just hoping to do my normal giant-robot attack, you know. Smash up a couple of buildings, have a fight, escape while cackling,

"You haven't heard the last of me!" At the very worst, encourage some low-level looting or let some animals escape from the zoo. I'd never plan anything like this, I swear!'

'So why are you telling us about it?' asked Doctor Extraordinary sternly.

'Well, this is kind of awkward,' said Captain Chaos, shuffling her feet. 'But I was rather hoping you might help me, you know . . .'

'You're going to have to say it,' prompted her arch-nemesis.

'Fine!' She looked at him with a slight smile. 'I need you to help me save Paragon City.'

Doctor Extraordinary broke into delighted laughter. 'Well, I've heard it all now,' he said, stooping to get his breath back. (Even though, being a ghost, he didn't actually have any breath.) 'You need to be prepared for anything as a superhero. I've always said it. But I was never quite ready for the day my greatest enemy would show up asking for my help in trying to disarm a huge explosive panda.'

'While we're both ghosts,' added Captain Chaos.

'Yes, while we're both ghosts,' said the doc. 'That does make it even weirder. But here we are. And there it is,' he added as a deep rumbling became audible from the direction of Paragon Park. 'Sonny, Spot, let's go!' he ordered, swishing his ghostly cloak as he turned and dashed back up the street.

The GIANT giant panda – which we know is, in fact, a GIANT giant bomb (a panda bomb, if you will) – had now reached the edge of Paragon Park. At the controls, PANDAmonium sniggered in crazed triumph as the enormous statue of Doctor Extraordinary came into view through the windscreen.

'Not far now, my black-and-white beauty,' she purred. 'Soon my evil plan will be complete, and Paragon City will be no more! A-ha-ha-ha-ha-haaaa!'

(You may have noticed a slight flaw in PANDAmonium's plan, which is that she will be in the GIANT giant panda when it explodes. Well, yes, that's true. But remember – and we really can't stress this fact enough – she's completely and utterly bananas.)

The panda flattened trees and bushes as it began

to stomp through the park. But then it met a line of resistance. Sonny's dad and his fellow officers had seen the hulking form approaching and realized they were facing a new threat. Forming well-organized lines, they charged forward to defend their city. It wasn't going to be easy – the small robot pandas who had been running away had now arranged themselves in formation on either side of the giant one, all of them edging forward like an army. Only, an army of pandas.

'Onward, brave men and women of the PCPD!' came a voice from away to one side. And the defenders of the city looked to see Doctor Extraordinary, now visible to all of them, arriving to lead the attack.

'This is the most important mission of your lives!' he told them. 'Your whole city depends on it. I'm nothing but a ghost so I'm afraid there's not much I can do. It's up to you to save Paragon City from now on – but you must STOP THAT PANDA!'

'STOP THAT PANDA! STOP THAT PANDA!' More and more of the crowd took up the battle cry.

Sonny's dad looked in trepidation at the huge shape of the approaching beast. As he watched, one of its huge feet stamped on a bandstand, instantly reducing it to flying splinters.

'We're going to have to bring in some heavy machinery to deal with that thing,' he said grimly, ducking inside his car and grabbing the radio. 'Control? This is Officer Nelson. Deploy all the armoured vehicles you've got in the north of Paragon Park.'

The handset crackled a question back at him.

'There's no time to chit-chat about it!' he snapped, his voice gaining a tone of authority it hadn't possessed for many years. 'Paragon City is in danger, and we're its only hope. Get those vehicles here. Now! Right, you lot!'

Putting down the radio, he darted out of the car and signalled to the rest of his squad. 'Attach the tow ropes to the back of your cars and follow me! Go for the legs!'

Sonny watched his dad with a warm rush of pride, a smile breaking out across his face.

Together the police cars sped in formation towards the enormous panda. At the last minute, they broke to either side, streaming towards its hind legs with their lights flashing and sirens blaring. As they passed, each officer threw out a tow rope attached to the back of

the car, before driving round and round the huge legs. Once the legs were lassoed, they drove as fast as possible backwards, attempting to drag the panda away from the museum.

In the control room, PANDAmonium laughed an even more crazed laugh than before. 'Fools!' she said and cackled. 'Do they really think their puny toy cars are a match for me and the might of my greatest creation, the GIANT giant panda?'

Sonny's dad was in the leading police car. 'Keep going!' he yelled out of the window as the tyres spun in the grass, digging deep, muddy trenches. 'We need to buy those armoured vehicles a bit of time!'

But gradually the police cars were being dragged backwards by the enormous robot. Sonny, strapped into the back seat, looked from side to side, hoping desperately that some kind of plan would occur to him. Suddenly a greyish glint from away to one side caught his eye.

'Dad!' he shouted. 'Look over there! The lake! What if we push the panda into it? Can they swim?'

His dad was wrestling with the steering wheel

frantically as the car fishtailed violently from side to side in the muddy grass. 'Are you seriously asking me whether pandas can swim?' he yelled back. 'Now? I'm a police officer, not a zookeeper!'

'You got a better idea?' his son asked.

'Fair enough,' Officer Nelson said with a sigh. 'It's got to be worth a try.'

Just then, the radio on the dashboard crackled.

'Nelson, Nelson, come in,' said a voice. 'Armoured cars are now in the area. Awaiting your instructions.'

Sonny's chest swelled with pride – everyone now seemed to be looking to his dad to tell them what to do. When the time had come, he'd stepped up. He was in charge.

'Form up and hit the panda from the side!' his dad instructed. 'We need to try and push it into the lake!'

'Can pandas swim?' asked the voice from the radio.

'Why does everyone keep asking me that?' said Officer Nelson crossly. 'I don't know whether pandas can swim or not, OK? Also, I don't think we should treat this as a normal panda – it's actually a giant robot. But, whatever – it's our only chance! We need to stop that thing from reaching the museum, or it's going to blow us all sky-high!'

There was a rumbling roar from away to one side, and a line of black armoured cars appeared, driving straight at the panda. With a clang, they slammed into its right hind leg, and slowly it began skidding to the left, towards the large ornamental boating lake. Ducks took flight in alarm as the enormous robot crashed through the trees and started to slide across the wooden boardwalk on the lake's edge.

'Keep going!' shouted Sonny's dad, half out of the car and straining to see what was going on. 'Looks like you've nearly got it in the water!'

PANDAmonium wrestled with the controls, trying to kick the vehicles away. But the hardware of the PCPD was too strong. With a grinding splosh, the GIANT giant panda was pushed into the lake, where it immediately sank without trace. There was a moment of silence as a few bubbles broke on the surface, and then the entire crowd broke into whoops and cheers.

'We did it!' said Sonny's dad in delight as the two of them raced towards the edge of the lake. 'We saved

Paragon City!'

Spot was already on the wooden boardwalk, looking doubtfully down at the water and ignoring the celebrating crowd surrounding her. Sonny dashed over to join her.

'Not feeling like celebrating just yet?' he asked.

Spot looked around. 'It's like these people have never read a book ever,' she told him. 'Don't they know that when the villain gets pushed into the water it's never the end?'

(Of course, Spot was absolutely right. You'd worked it out for yourself, though, hadn't you? There's a chapter and a half still to go. You didn't think this was the end, did you? Good – cos it's not.)

The cheers from the crowd suddenly died away as more and more bubbles appeared on the lake. With them came a series of deep ripples and a very disturbing rumbling noise. There was a stampede away from the boardwalk, but only just in time. The GIANT giant panda burst from the lake, water streaming from its head and sides. Roaring, it swiped left and right with its front paws, sending the armoured cars somersaulting away like skittles.

'Did you think it would be that easy to stop me?' yelled PANDAmonium in the control room. 'Well, think again!

This is one panda who refuses to be endangered!'

Nobody could hear because the room was soundproof, but she shouted it anyway. Supervillains love shouting. Wrenching the control lever to the left, she steered the huge robot panda back towards the museum.

Sonny and Spot watched helplessly as the enormous machine lurched away from them.

'That's it, then,' said Sonny sadly. 'We did our best, but I just don't see how anybody can stop that thing.'

And then the panda bomb reached the museum and exploded.

THE END

Ha ha! Not really. Had you going for a moment, though, didn't we?
Only kidding. This is what actually happened:

Doctor Extraordinary came hurrying towards them.
'Spot! Sonny!' he was calling, waving his arms excitedly.
'I think I have a plan! This is very exciting! It's usually
Lana who comes up with them, but I've had one of my
own! Maybe not having superpowers any more has given
me more thinking time!'

'What plan have you had, Doc?' said Spot, breaking
into this monologue before it got out of hand.

'Ah yes!' Doctor Extraordinary faced them with a huge
grin. 'Well, you know that panda is powered by Q energy?
That's why it'll explode when it reaches the museum.'

'Yes!' said Sonny impatiently, glancing at the giant
panda, which was already vanishing among the trees.
'Stop summarizing the plot so far. There isn't time!
What's the plan?'

'Well,' said the doc, looking very pleased with himself,
'if we destroy the Q crystals in the museum, that can't
happen, can it? We could use Lana's prototype weapon,
remember? The one you saw at Extraordinary HQ!'

(BARRY'S BADGER ALERT.)

At that moment, a voice crackled from the walkie-talkie on Sonny's belt.

'Doc, come in!' said the voice of Professor Lana Holliday. 'Do you read me? I think that if you use my prototype weapon you might be able to destroy the Q crystals!'

Sonny grabbed the handset and pressed the transmit button, holding it up so the doc could speak.

'For once, Holliday,' he said, 'I'm slightly ahead of you. We've just hit on the exact same plan. Prepare the prototype, attach it to the Extra-Jet and ready it for take-off!'

'Roger, wilco,' confirmed Lana Holliday. 'But hurry! There's no time to lose!'

'She's not wrong,' muttered Sonny, glancing over at the GIANT giant panda, now only a few hundred metres away from the museum and the Q crystals inside. 'This way!' he shouted to the doc, beckoning him towards a nearby police helicopter.

For a moment, Sonny thought he wasn't going to be able to convince the officers on board the helicopter to take him out to Extraordinary Island. But as he approached, yelling, 'Get ready for take-off! We can still save the city!', he was relieved to hear one of them say, 'Hey, that's Nelson's kid! The one from the TV! Good job, son!'

'Thanks,' gasped Sonny as the woman hauled him up through a side door into the cabin. 'But there's no time! We need to get out to the island – it's the only way to save the city!'

Before long, they were zooming low across the lake, with the main white HQ building growing larger through the windscreen as the pilot urged the chopper forward.

308

But, as the silvery lake zipped by beneath them, a thought hit Sonny that made him feel like a lead weight had suddenly materialized just beneath his stomach.

'Hang on,' he told Doctor Extraordinary, who was staring out of the window back towards the city. 'If I understood Lana's little science lesson properly . . . aren't the Q crystals the only thing that's keeping you in this dimension? The only reason you're still here?'

'Ah, yes,' the doc replied without turning round. 'I was wondering whether you might realize that.'

'So if we destroy them,' Sonny went on, 'you won't be a ghost any more. You'll disappear.'

'From this dimension, yes,' said the doc. 'I'll disappear from your view, it's true. But I'll still exist out there somewhere. No idea what that'll be like. But, after all, I've been feeling for quite a while that it might be time for a new adventure. I was wishing only the other week that Paragon City would save itself for once. And now, it seems, Paragon City is perfectly capable of doing that. You might almost say that my work here is done.'

The enormity of it hit Sonny like a tidal wave. But, somewhere beneath the slosh of cold shock, there was a glimmer of understanding and of acceptance. Part of him realized that this was the perfect ending – the only possible ending – to the incredible story of Doctor Extraordinary. His hero would save Paragon City one last time, once and for all. And then both he and Captain Chaos would vanish to some other realm, somewhere out there in the unseen parts of the universe. Leaving behind a city that could now defend itself.

'My greatest mission,' said the doc as if reading his thoughts and finally turning away from the window to meet Sonny's eye. 'And I can think of no finer hero to face it with.'

CHAPTER 13
GIVING UP THE GHOST

Sonny Nelson had spent hours dreaming about flying across Paragon City with Doctor Extraordinary. He'd imagined his hero waving to the crowds below as they swooped low over the city's wide avenues, the bright green splash of Paragon Park with the statue towering above it visible in the distance. But he'd never once thought that it might be under these circumstances. Because here he was, right there in that long-imagined Extra-Jet cockpit, as the superhero flew past the city he had protected for one final time.

There were indeed crowds below them. Crowds of people who had turned out to help defend their city against the panda invasion. Crowds of people who – while conveniently dressed as superheroes for the Hero Day parade – had actually turned themselves into protectors of Paragon City. And they had discovered that, as they did so, they were finally able to see the ghost of their once-resident superhero.

They cheered and punched the air as the Extra-Jet roared overhead. And, just like in Sonny's dreams, the doc was waving to them out of the window. But what none of the cheering people below knew was that he was actually waving goodbye.

Professor Lana Holliday, who was also squeezed rather uncomfortably into the jet's cockpit, had been aghast when she realized what Doctor Extraordinary's plan would mean. 'But . . . but . . .' she had sputtered. 'You'll disappear! You won't be a ghost any more! I don't know what will happen to you!'

'Didn't you tell Spot that the best thing a scientist can ever do is discover a brand-new mystery, Holliday?' the doc had asked, placing a calming hand on her shoulder even though she couldn't feel it.

'I suppose I did,' replied the professor, wiping away

yet another unscientific tear.

And so now, with the prototype weapon fastened securely beneath the jet, they were on their way to carry out Doctor Extraordinary's final mission. Well, final in this particular dimension anyway. The weapon would destroy the mysterious space crystals that had given the doc his powers. The ones that had rendered him indestructible, and kept him in the city as a ghost. But those Q crystals were also about to completely destroy everything he had spent the last twenty years defending. It was time to go.

As the jet approached the Doctor Extraordinary Museum, Sonny – instructed by the doc – eased back the joystick to slow it down. Several figures were visible on the concrete roof, clustered round a large circular metal case. Spot and Sonny's dad, helped by several of his fellow officers, had brought the Q crystals out into the open while the multicoloured figure of Captain Chaos fussed round them, gesturing towards the GIANT giant panda in panic.

It was clear there was no time to waste: the huge walking bomb was now frighteningly close and drawing nearer every second. It was close enough for Sonny to make out a pale black-eyed face in the control room on top of its head. Even from this distance, it was obvious that PANDAmonium was grinning and cackling in triumph.

We'll see about that, thought Sonny grimly as he steered the jet in to land on an empty section of the roof.

But even through his sadness and determination he wasn't able to tamp down a tiny flare of excitement and pride that he was actually landing the Extra-Jet by himself. At least Spot seemed to realize what a big deal it was – he could see her capering and pointing in excitement. He returned her beaming smile as the jet thunked smoothly down on the roof, and the roar of the engines began to wind down.

Pushing back the cockpit roof, Sonny jumped out on to the smooth black surface of the wing. 'Doc, let's go!'

Doctor Extraordinary was still in the co-pilot's chair, staring into the distance. At Sonny's words, he gave a slight shake of his head and fixed a rather fake-looking expression of calm determination on to his face.

'You've got it,' he told his number-one fan. 'Never say

die! Let's finish this panda invasion once and for all!' He broke into a watery smile. 'You know what? I just can't *bear* it.'

Not only had Sonny just flown the Extra-Jet on a vital rescue mission, now he was getting to exchange quips with an actual superhero. Even though that hero was about to vanish. It was simultaneously the worst and the best afternoon ever.

'Let's obliterate the crystals before the whole city goes bam-boom!' he suggested.

'Not bad,' the doc said as he climbed out of the Extra-Jet for the last time ever. 'You know what? You're rather good at the old superhero quips. Yet another sign that I'm leaving the city in safe hands.'

His eyes strayed to the assembled police officers on the roof and the citizens below, many of them still bravely battling the small panda robots.

Doctor Extraordinary stood beside the Extra-Jet, his eyes fixed on the approaching panda and the manic eyes of its pilot. At the same time, he was aware of a blur of bright colours beside him as Captain Chaos joined him.

'Catherine,' he said formally.

'Xavier.'

'You know what this will mean?' he asked her. She nodded, staring at the case of glowing crystals throwing their eerie bluey-white light into the darkening afternoon sky.

'Who knew that it was your sidekick who would turn out to be the real villain all along?' asked the doc wryly. 'It appears neither of us really won in the end.'

'Well, that hasn't been decided yet, has it?' she said, smiling a sly smile. 'After all, I'm sure that wherever we're going there'll be lots more chaos to cause. Who's going to be there to stop me?'

'I am!' said the doc happily. 'I suppose the quantum realm needs defending, right? Now that Paragon City seems to be learning to look after itself at last.'

'Darned straight it does,' Captain Chaos told him. 'I'm going to cause absolute havoc out there. You'd better be ready, Doc.'

Hero and villain turned to each other with a peculiar expression: one third determination, one third a smile and one third a mixture of emotions that there just aren't words for. A single tear glinted briefly at the corner of

Doctor Extraordinary's eye, but he blinked it away.

Superheroes don't cry, he thought. *Or maybe they do. I'm still learning how to do this.*

'Ready?' Professor Lana Holliday, accompanied by Sonny and Spot, had moved to stand beside them.

At that moment, there a splintering crash as the GIANT giant panda broke through the high fence surrounding the museum gardens. It was now mere metres away, and the light from the Q crystals began to intensify, pulsating with an unearthly glow and throwing out blasts of intense heat.

'Ready or not,' said Doctor Extraordinary, 'there's no time to lose. Go for it, Holliday!'

Lana flipped up a panel on the side of the prototype and pulled down a large lever. There was a descending whine and a clanking noise. Rows of coloured lights blinked on along the side of the missile-shaped device, then flashed off again.

'It's not working!' said Lana between gritted teeth, jiggling the lever up and down. The air was full of the thundering noise of the panda's footsteps.

'Just . . . I don't know . . .' Doctor Extraordinary caught

Captain Chaos's eye and broke into a grin. 'Just have a poke about or something!'

'Have a poke about?' repeated his former assistant, returning the grin as she remembered that day long ago when both their lives had changed. 'That's not very scientific!'

'Oh, you can't always be scientific about everything, you know!' said a voice. And Spot, clenching her fist, gave the prototype weapon a huge punch that made the whole jet vibrate with a deep clang.

At once, the lights blinked back into life. 'Target calibrated,' said a calm electronic voice. 'Commencing disintegration.'

A high-pitched whining filled the rooftop, and several of the police officers clamped their hands over their ears. The heat from the Q crystals was becoming hard to bear. Sonny reached up his hands to protect his face, squinting his eyes against the bright light.

As almost everybody on the rooftop cowered away from the heat and the noise, two lone figures stood calmly and proudly in the blinding light.

Captain Chaos gazed into the heart of the Q crystals

as they began to shimmer and dissolve. And beside her, Doctor Extraordinary took one last look out across the city that he had protected for two decades. He turned his head to take in the bright waters of the lake. He saw the buildings of Paragon City and the dark shapes of the mountains beyond. And our hero stood for a final moment, caught – as we all are – in a moment between sunrise and shadow.

And then the noise, the light and the heat built up to a final crescendo. The Q crystals collapsed into a fine dust that was whipped into whirlpools and borne away by the fresh breeze. And, as the fine dust disappeared, so too the ghosts on the rooftop began to fade. Sonny's dad wrapped an arm round his son's shoulder as Doctor Extraordinary faced them.

'I think I can see what's out there,' said the doc, staring off to one side. 'And I think this is going to be very, very interesting.'

'Before you go,' said Sonny, barely holding it together, but feeling that breaking down in tears at this moment would be something of a waste, 'I just wanted to say, you know . . . thanks. From me, but also from all of us.'

319

With a wave of his arm, he indicated Spot, the rest of the crowd on the rooftop and the people below, all of them now staring up at the bright blue light beaming into the sky.

'It should really be me thanking you,' said the doc. 'What would I have done without you, eh? The only person who could see me. Because you were the only one who really, truly believed.' He gave Sonny's dad a wink. 'Look after the old place for me, won't you?' he asked. 'You're the heroes now.'

Sonny's dad gave a smart salute. 'You know it,' he replied.

By now, Doctor Extraordinary was little more than a vague shadow.

'Good to know I'm leaving things in safe hands,' came a muted voice – hardly more than a whisper on the wind. Only four more words were audible – faint and far away.

'Onward to the unknown,' said the hero of Paragon City as he disappeared.

In the control room of the GIANT giant panda, PANDAmonium rocked backwards and forward, hooting in glee as the huge robot lumbered the last few metres towards the Doctor Extraordinary Museum.

She could see a crowd gathered on the rooftop, but paid them no attention. She was only focused on the pulsing light that had started to fill the air: a light that could only mean one thing. The Q energy from the meteorite had begun to activate as the panda drew closer. In mere seconds, the energy of the panda and the energy from the crystals would combine, creating an explosion that would leave nothing but a smoking crater where Paragon City had once been.

A slightly worrying thought occurred to her at this point. *Hang on*, said the slightly worrying thought. *You're going to be right in the middle of the explosion. You'll be wiped out, too.*

'Meh,' said PANDAmonium out loud. 'Who cares?' She really was off her rocker.

The control room began to fill with dazzling light as the crystals got even nearer. But something else seemed to be happening at the same time. Something that didn't feel in the least bit *'mwah-ha-ha, my evil plan has come to fruition'*. It felt a great deal more like *'curses, my evil plan has been foiled at the last minute*', which is something that supervillains really, really hate.

The GIANT giant panda began to falter and judder, lights blinked crazily on the control panel, and a robotic voice began to drone: `SYSTEM FAILURE. SYSTEM FAILURE. CRYSTAL ENERGY FAILING.`

'*Whaaaaat?*' screeched PANDAmonium, mashing buttons in a frenzy.

But it was no use. A mere two steps away from the museum wall, the panda sank to its knees as if it had been hit with a tranquillizer dart. With a descending drone as all its engines shut down, it slumped further to the ground, and the control-room window sprang open. PANDAmonium looked up to see herself surrounded by dozens of Paragon City police officers, all glaring at her furiously.

One of them stepped forward. 'I'm guessing you're the one behind all the panda stuff?' said Officer Dusty Nelson as his son watched him from the sidelines, bursting with pride.

He looked at her black-and-white clothes, her white face with the black rings under the eyes and – most tellingly – the large badge saying **I ♥ PANDAS** pinned to the lapel of her jacket.

'Hands-a behind your back, panda lady,' Dusty went on, holding out a finger with a gleaming set of handcuffs dangling from it.

'You don't get to do quips!' said PANDAmonium indignantly. 'Quips are for superheroes!'

'Oh, didn't you get the memo?' Dusty replied as he cuffed her hands behind her back, gesturing out across the crowds of Paragonians spread below them, all in their Hero Day fancy dress. 'We're all superheroes today.'

A barrage of camera flashes went off as Sonny and his dad, arms wrapped round each other's shoulders, stumbled out of the front door of the museum.

'Officer Nelson! Officer Nelson!' yelled Ben Bailey, who was right in the middle of the press pack. 'Any words for our viewers? What would you say to the people of Paragon City?'

'I think I'd just say well done,' said Sonny's dad with a smile. 'Because I think that, for the first time in a very, very long time, Paragon City just saved itself.'

'And what would you say to people who are calling you a hero?' asked Ben, pushing further forward and sticking his microphone under their noses.

'Well, how many people live in Paragon City?'

Ben Bailey was ready with the answer. 'Just over six million at the last count, I believe,' he replied.

'Well, in that case,' Sonny's dad went on, 'if I'm a hero, then I'm one of six million of them. Including you, Ben. I saw you giving quite a few of those pandas a run for their money.'

'Well, Susie, there you have it,' said Ben Bailey, turning to the camera. 'Heroes everywhere. And, let's face it, we learned from the best. Doctor Extraordinary, wherever you are, if you can hear this . . . I think we all just want to say thank you.'

The crowd around him broke into applause.

Sonny turned to Spot as they slipped quietly away. 'I suppose our temporary arrangement is at an end, then?' he said.

She crinkled her nose in puzzlement. 'What?'

'Well, if you remember,' he told her, 'you wanted a temporary arrangement where we'd hang out so you could gather more data about my . . . what was the word? My *delusion* that I could see the ghost of Doctor Extraordinary.'

'Oh. Ah.' Spot shook her hair forward over her face awkwardly. 'That. Yes.'

'So I guess you have all the data you need, right?'

'*We-e-ell*,' she said with the beginnings of a sly grin, 'it wouldn't be strictly scientific to end things so abruptly. I mean, we should really discuss what we discovered. Over, you know . . . doughnuts or something.'

'You want to be friends!' said Sonny, pointing at her.

'I don't!' Spot protested hotly. 'Friendship is highly unscientific, remember? Well, maybe I could make an exception,' she said. 'As we did just save the entire city and everything.'

She held out a hand and Sonny shook it firmly.

'Friends,' she said, the grin she'd started earlier now breaking out over her entire face like a sunrise.

'Did I just hear someone mentioning doughnuts?' came a voice from behind them.

They turned to see Sonny's dad and Lana Holliday hurrying away from the crowd.

326

'Sounds like a plan to me,' Officer Dusty went on. 'Doughnut date tomorrow morning, fellow saviours of Paragon City? When we've all got cleaned up a bit.'

Sonny looked round at his friends, noticing for the first time that their clothes were filthy, smeared with grime and scorched by the light and heat from the Q crystals.

'Doughnut date it is,' agreed Sonny, Spot and Lana.

The following morning, Sonny's dad poked his head round the bedroom door to find his son taking down his numerous posters and articles about Doctor Extraordinary, and stacking them on the bed.

'Redecorating?' he asked.

Sonny turned and smiled. 'Hey, Dad. You look smart!'

His father's police uniform looked freshly ironed. His belt buckle and cap badge shone with polish.

'Well, seems like it'll be a big day at work,' his dad said. 'I've been called in to meet the mayor. There's even talk of a promotion.'

'Talking of a promotion,' said Sonny, 'how about this?'

He held up a newspaper – the front page of that day's *Paragon Herald*. It bore a large black-and-white picture of the two of them in front of the museum, looking battle-scarred and grubby, but undoubtedly very heroic.

DEFENDERS OF PARAGON CITY!

said the headline – and, in smaller letters underneath:

PANDA PANDAMONIUM AVOIDED!

'What about the doc?' asked his dad.

'Page two,' Sonny replied. 'Pretty impressive stuff, Dad. You've actually pushed a real-life superhero off the front page of the newspaper. And that's why –' he turned and pinned the front page to his wall – 'you get pride of place. Listen to what they wrote about you!'

Grabbing another page, he read out loud. '*Paragon City has a new hero today. One that doesn't wear a costume or fly in a supercharged jet. One that doesn't have super strength or super speed . . .*'

'Stop it!' Blushing slightly, his dad cut him off. 'You don't want to pay too much attention to the nonsense they write,' he said awkwardly. 'Besides, you were the real hero. Who else believed in the doc?'

'It wasn't about believing in Doctor Extraordinary,'

Sonny told him. 'It was about realizing we didn't need him. In a way, it was about not believing in him! And finding out that we didn't need a superhero to keep saving us. We just needed to learn to save ourselves.'

'This is all starting to sound too much like the end of a film for my liking,' said his dad, laughing. 'Come on – the others will be waiting!'

Sonny and his father walked out of the block of flats together and into the busy crowds of Paragon City spread out beside the sparkling waters of Lake Sunrise. As they crossed the street, something made Sonny turn and look back up at his building. There, in her wide window, was Miss Abigail. Smiling, she was holding up her patchwork quilt, the map of the city catching the morning light. Sonny gave her a huge thumbs up.

'Looks like it's finished at last,' he told his dad as they turned to carry on across the road, where he could see Spot and Lana waiting.

'Dad's off to see the mayor later,' Sonny told them proudly as they approached.

'That's a coincidence,' said Lana. 'So am I! She's asking whether I might help the police department out

with some new technology. I think it's safe to say that we're going to be pretty busy out at Extraordinary HQ.' She raised her eyebrows. 'So much so, in fact, that I've had to take on a brand-new assistant.'

Beside her, Sonny saw Spot swell with pride.

'That's incredible!' he said.

'Don't you mean extraordinary?' she corrected.

And so the defenders of Paragon City set off through the busy streets in search of doughnuts.

The wide blue sky stretched out across the city to the dark mountains beyond. And, high above, a wisp of cloud floated along, lonely in the vast emptiness. It was strangely shaped; if you squinted, it almost looked like the figure of a man, unimaginably high up and far away. A man with a flowing cape, smiling out across the city as he held out an upraised thumb in a gesture of triumph.

But Sonny Nelson was too deep in conversation with his dad and his friends to notice it.

THE END

ACKNOWLEDGEMENTS

With huge THANKS to the following superheroes:

Carmen McCullough. Hero name: The Editron. Superpower: X-ray plot vision.

Amy Nguyen. Hero name: Kid Scribbles. Superpower: can make pictures come alive.

Pippa Shaw. Hero name: The Fists of Grammar (and her proofreading sidekicks). Superpower: making repeated words explode.

Andrea Kearney. Hero name: Design-o-Bot. Superpower: panda placement.

Amanda and Ruth, Lizz, Charlotte, Stevie and Riana, Alice and Zosia – all the other members of the Super Puffins. Superpowers: flying around clifftops with their tiny stubby wings.

Stephanie Thwaites. Hero name: Agent Kickass. Superpower: posh lunch and sympathetic ears.

ACKNOWLEDGEMENTS

Coldplay very kindly let us use their lyrics at the front of the book so massive thanks to Chris, Will, Guy, Jonny and Phil – what they don't know is that we added some small print to the contract that means they are now legally bound to do the soundtrack for the film version. Cheers, guys. And welcome aboard!

We also need to give a very special mention to the wonderful city of Chicago for making us so welcome and becoming the inspiration for Paragon City.

And thanks to Zoom. We couldn't have written this book without you, but we never want to see you ever again.

SPECIAL THANKS FROM GREG to Bella and Barney for being incredibly fun pals – I'm very lucky to have you both by my side when the world gets too much. I'd also like to thank Gregg Wallace for being Gregg Wallace.

SPECIAL THANKS FROM CHRIS to Jenny and Lucas – love you both. And to Mabel the cat – as a special thanks to you, the first copies of this book will be delivered in a large cardboard box which you can sit in looking oddly proud like a total weirdo.

DID YOU LOVE *SUPER GHOST*?

THEN YOU'LL DEFINITELY LOVE

THE GREAT DREAM ROBBERY.

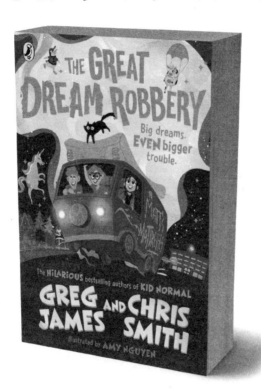

Here's a sneak peek of this adventure
beyond your WILDEST DREAMS!

CHAPTER 1
THE STRANGER IN THE DREAM

'Ten minutes! Come on, please – just another ten minutes!'

'No!'

'Oh . . . *please*! All right, then – five minutes. Just five more minutes!'

'No, I told you already. It's bedtime! There's school tomorrow.'

'Yeah, but there aren't any really important lessons. Not in the morning anyway. Go on . . . just another five minutes. **Pleeeeeeeeeease?**'

'Mum . . . no! I really need to get to bed.'

'Oh, come on, Maya. You can sit up with me for another five minutes, surely?'

Maya Clayton stopped at the bottom of the stairs and huffed with frustration. Behind her, her mum sat cross-legged on the sofa cradling a mug of hot chocolate in both hands. Maya hesitated – it all looked very warm and inviting. But Maya had two very particular reasons why she didn't want to sit up chatting to her mum.

The first reason was an invisible force field of sadness that made the room much less inviting than it seemed at first glance. Looking past her mum, Maya could visualize it quite clearly, stirring the air like a chilly draught. It radiated out from an empty armchair next to the sofa. It was the chair where her father – Professor Dexter Clayton – would normally have been sitting, until the terrible accident six weeks ago.

The second reason why Maya Clayton was desperate to get to bed is harder to explain but all the more interesting for it. For dramatic reasons, we're not going to tell you about it until later in the chapter, but it's worth waiting for, we promise.

Maya's eyes lingered on the vacant chair and her mum followed her gaze. 'He'll be back sitting there before you know it,' she promised, though it was hard to tell who she was trying to convince. 'I know you miss him. Come on. Come and sit with me for a bit. It might help to talk about it, you know.'

Maya – who had taken a tentative step back into the room – hesitated. She didn't want to talk. How could she possibly express all the things she was feeling right now? Some things are just too sad for words to do them justice.

Seeing her expression change, her mum back-pedalled: 'OK, OK! No talking necessary. Look, we can just sit and watch telly.' She clicked the remote.

Tinkly music immediately filled the room, along with a strident, nasal voice: 'Hoo hoo! Evening, sleepyheads!' Maya and her mum groaned in unison.

'Worst advert EVER!'

warned Maya. 'Quick – change channels!' But in a frantic race to comply, her mum fumbled the remote, batting it upward and away, and it scuttled under the empty chair like a rat with stage fright.

The tinkly music continued, intending to sound soothing but actually sounding like the part in a horror film just before a clown jumps out at you. Then a man appeared on-screen, dressed in an old-fashioned nightgown and cap and holding a candle. 'Bedtime!' he exclaimed into the camera. 'And when you think bedtime – think of Matt! That's me – the owner of Matt's Mattresses!' He winked, prompting another joint groan from Maya and her mum. This advert seemed to be showing every time they turned on the TV and their hatred of it had become a running joke – a way of cheering themselves up during the bleak weeks as they readjusted to a house with only the two of them in it.

'That's a sign from the gods of bad telly,' Maya told her mum decisively, beginning to turn away. 'It is definitely bedtime.'

'Hang on, I'll change it!' Slopping hot chocolate on her fingers, her mum shuffled over to the empty chair and began to search for the remote. 'Give me literally eight seconds.'

Watching her, Maya felt a sudden pang of pity. She wasn't the only person affected by the invisible sadness field, she thought to herself. This was tough on both of them. She hurried over and kneeled to give her mum a quick hug. 'Thanks,' she said, forcing a smile. 'But I'm really heading to bed. I'm wiped out.'

'It's not normal, you know.' Her mum smiled at her. 'A twelve-year-old who wants to go to bed early.'

'Yeah, well, remember what Dad always says?' Maya replied, glancing once again at the empty armchair. 'Who wants to be normal?'

'Fair point,' her mum agreed, breaking off the hug. 'Sleep well. Sweet dreams.'

Maya, who'd been edging away, paused briefly at this. It flitted across her mind that maybe she should talk to her mum some more about the dream she'd had the previous night. But the man in the nightcap on TV was now burbling, 'Matt's Mattresses are the

only mattresses with the revolutionary Flamewood
Floaty Foam! Formulated by phenomenal physicists,
Flamewood Floaty Foam is fashioned from the finest
fibres. When you flop on to Flamewood Floaty Foam,
you'll feel fantastic!' The irritating voice receded as Maya
stumped up the stairs. Reaching the top, she ducked
into the bathroom, cutting the man off mid spiel –

'Floaty Foam!
It's famous!
It's fashionable!
It's f–'

by slamming the door firmly behind her.

The bathroom window looked out on to the Claytons'
garden, lit up with the brownish glow of a cloudy, late
spring evening. As Maya gazed out of the window while
brushing her teeth, a lone ray of sunlight escaped like a
pointing finger to land on the large wooden workshop
at the end of the garden. Maya released a mint-
scented sigh. This long, low building with its cluttered

workbenches was where she and her father had spent countless happy hours together. Professor Dexter would usually be busy with piles of paper or a laptop, sitting at his large desk beneath a lit-up neon sign. The sign consisted of six letters – his favourite letters in the entire language, the professor was fond of saying. They spelled out the simple words:

What if?

'The most important question you can ever ask,' he would tell Maya.

He'd set one wall of the workshop aside as Maya's special area. From right back when she was tiny, she had loved to draw. That was what had earned her the nickname used by her father and nobody else – Scribbles. When her teachers complained about exercise books filled with pages and pages of doodles, her father had stood up for her. 'It's just the way her brain works,' he'd explained during one parents' evening, 'and we should never stop a brain from working.' That very night, when they got home, he painted one wall of his workshop white, just for Scribbles, and designated it her Doodle Wall. She had spent hours covering it with fantastical landscapes and creatures: castles, unicorns, spaceships . . . Years of imagination filled the whitewashed planks, all in Maya's thin, spidery style. Now, peering out of the bathroom window, she could dimly make out some of her doodles caught in the evening sunlight. She stared until her eyes prickled, wishing with all her heart that her father was sitting there as he always had done, beneath the sign reading WHAT IF?

Maya heard a loud purring from behind her and turned to see a large and extremely scruffy black cat sitting on the bathroom stool, regarding her calmly with wide green eyes.

'I bet you miss him too, don't you, Bin Bag?' Maya asked the cat, scratching him behind one ear. She had come up with his name when she was small, for the very simple reason that if you scrumpled up a large black bin bag and placed bag and cat side by side, you'd be hard-pressed to tell the difference. No matter how much you groomed him, he always looked untidy and windswept, rather like the hair of a child wizard.

Bin Bag purred even more loudly and followed her into the bedroom, where she changed into her pyjamas and dived beneath her duvet with the grace of a greased penguin slipping beneath an ice floe. Her head was bepillowed and her eyes shut before her black T-shirt – which had been thrown into the air during pyjamarization – had drifted to rest on a nearby chair.

As her mum had quite correctly pointed out, it's not often you find a twelve-year-old as keen to go to bed as Maya Clayton. But that particular night she had a very specific reason for wanting to get to sleep as soon as possible. It was all to do with the dream she'd had the previous night. A very vivid and extremely strange dream that had ended on a very intriguing and extremely annoying cliffhanger. And it had been all about her dad.